Murder At 1

By

Anya Wylde

Copyright 2014 Anya Wylde

Acknowledgement

Husband, I know this is a touchy topic but hair or no hair, I still love you.

Mother, thank you very much for giving birth to me. You did well.

Contents

Acknowledgement

Chapter 1

Chapter 2

Chapter 3

Chapter 4

Chapter 5

Chapter 6

Chapter 7

Chapter 8

Chapter 9

Chapter 10

Chapter 11

Chapter 12

Chapter 13

Chapter 14

Chapter 15

Chapter 16

Chapter 17

Chapter 18

Chapter 19

Chapter 20

Chapter 21

Chapter 22

Chapter 23

Chapter 24

Chapter 25

Chapter 26

Chapter 27

Chapter 28

Chapter 29

Chapter 30

Chapter 31

Chapter 32

Chapter 33

Chapter 34

Chapter 35

Chapter 36

About the Author

Chapter 1

"Miss Trotter, I hope you understand what an honour this is?"

"Yes, Miss Summer," Lucy replied meekly.

"You will be stepping out into the world and leaving the comforts of this orphanage forever. You will be representing us, Miss Trotter, in an aristocratic family, and I hope you will do nothing to tarnish our good name."

"No, Miss Summer."

"We have fed you, clothed you and educated you. You were one of the privileged young women allowed to take lessons in French, History and Latin instead of being trained to scrub fireplaces or work in a mill."

"Yes, Miss Summer."

"Do you know why you were allowed such advantages?"

"No, Miss Summer."

"Because you have something rare, something that is lacking in over half of the world's population. It is a thing so beautiful that I cannot ignore it when I see it."

"Truly, Miss Summer?"

"Yes, Miss Trotter. You have that something rare and precious, commonly known as a brain. And I have met very few brains in my life, my dear. Most have been pulpy, frothy or entirely empty. But not yours. Oh, no, no, no . . . *your* upper story is remarkable. It is well-oiled, functioning and above all, sparkling." The dark eyes above full pink cheeks narrowed. "But that does not mean you are devoid of faults."

"No, Miss Summer."

"At the Brooding Cranesbill we have tried our best to cleanse you of your peccadilloes, but I can see we have not completely succeeded." The old teacher moved forward in her seat, and the silver streaks in her scraped back hair glinted in the light. "Are you certain, child, that you wouldn't rather work for the doctor? He said you were good at making healing salves and never so much as squealed at the sight of blood. His patients like you—"

"I want to be a governess, miss."

"Well, then, if you are certain?" At Lucy's firm nod, she continued. "You do not squeal at the sight of blood, but you do squeal at the sight of ribbons. You must curtail this pleasure in frivolous things."

"Yes, Miss Summer."

"You will remember at all times that you are an adult now. You cannot play with the children as if they are your equal or behave in any childish manner."

"I won't forget, Miss Summer—"

Once again, Miss Summer leaned forward in her seat, arresting Lucy's tongue. "You won't change your mind? I can let you take care of the young children here at the orphanage. I will even pay you, not as much as Lord Sedley is offering but close enough. You are hardworking, intelligent and, truth be told, I am afraid of letting you run around England—"

"I am certain," Lucy replied with another firm nod.

"But the children are eight and ten years old. The last time you were asked to take care of a group of children that age, we found the lot five miles south hanging out of apple trees."

"I was young—"

"It happened three months ago."

"I promise I won't encourage the children under my charge to steal from farmers ever again—"

"You encouraged them to steal?" Miss Summer reeled back, a hand on her scandalised heart.

"No, I mean I simply mentioned that the farmer seemed to have had a good year and one apple each wouldn't hurt him. If birds can peck on them and ruin—"

"Miss Trotter, you shall not steal. Not from farmers or from the kitchens. Let ants and bloody birds have it if they want."

"Yes, Miss Summer," she replied with a heartfelt sigh.

As expected, the sigh immediately softened the old lady. "You are a good girl—talented, charming, friendly, well-liked . . . If only you didn't have a gap in your front teeth, you would have been considered attractive."

Lucy pressed her lips together to hide the offending teeth.

Miss Summer tapped the table thoughtfully, her eyes scanning a very long list in front of her. "What else? Ah yes, do not rearrange Lord Sedley's library as you did for us when you were fifteen. It is not amusing. And don't even think of wriggling down a creeper. You have an odd fear of heights. It comes on like hiccups. Most of the time you scale down the wall and sneak off to the nearest village like an experienced crook, but when the fear hits you," She shook a finger in warning, "you stop midway hanging four feet above the ground, clutching a bit of ivy, swinging to and fro with your eyes closed shivering like a furless polar bear—"

"I will be good, Miss Summer. I truly will."

Miss Summer pushed the list away. "Will you?" she asked sceptically. "Or rather, can you be good for an extended period, Miss Trotter? I suppose I cannot tie you to the chair you are currently warming and keep you here forever . . . ."

Lucy nervously shook her head.

"It won't be easy," Miss Summer warned.

"The world is full of dangers," Lucy agreed. "I will be careful."

"It won't be easy," Miss Summer repeated firmly, "for the world to adjust to your presence. England will have to shift around, make space, adapt a little, stand on its toenails and stay alert to be able to absorb someone like you . . . It may happen . . . Miracles are not unheard off."

Lucy fixed her eye on a white speck on the table.

Miss Summer rummaged around in her desk drawer. "Your mother's sister regretted the fact that she couldn't take you in after your parents died in the fire, but she had eleven grimy ones of her own. Here." She handed a deep red pouch to Lucy, "She left you some money. She wanted me to give it to you when you were old enough. I would have preferred waiting a little longer before giving it to you, but age seems to define wisdom for some fools."

Lucy jingled the pouch. It wasn't much, but at least it was something.

"It may be enough to buy you a dress," Miss Summer said jerking a round dimpled chin towards the pouch. "Now, for the last time, Miss Lucy Anne Trotter, are you certain you want to go to Blackwell and take care of the children in Rudhall Manor?"

"I won't change my mind, Miss Summer."

"Well, then, that is that."

"Yes, that is that."

"That is final?"

"It is."

"You will not be allowed back once you leave, Miss Trotter. You are aware we have responsibilities, many mouths to feed—"

"I understand."

"I see . . . This is goodbye then."

"Yes," Lucy said in a voice thick with emotion. "Goodbye, Miss Summer." She paused near the door and looked back at her beloved teacher. "And, Miss Summer . . ."

"Yes?"

"Thank you . . . for everything."

"You are welcome, child. Now repay me by behaving like a well-mannered young lady for the rest of your life."

"I shall try my best, Miss Summer."

"For Lord Sedley's sake, I truly hope so."

Lucy nodded and left the room. She closed the door and leaned back against it.

After a brief moment, she opened one dark brown eye and looked right and left.

The corridor was empty.

Her ears strained and twitched.

All was silent.

Her lips curled up at the corners, and then as if a bee stung her arm, she jerked and came alive. Her arm began flapping, her legs began hopping, and her head shook from side to side. Her pins flew into the air, and her thick brown locks loosened and knotted themselves together.

She did not notice when the door opened behind her and Miss Summer came out, nor did she see when the nearest room emptied, and a group of sixteen-year-olds abandoned their stitching to come and watch her.

ANYA WYLDE

Nor did she stop when a distant dinner bell peeled through the orphanage because, at this beautiful moment, Miss Lucy Anne Trotter was busy doing the happy dance of freedom.

Chapter 2

Three months later . . .

On the outskirts of London, wedged between Muffly and Duffly, sat a quiet village called Blackwell.

And while London leapt, bounded and raced about, Blackwell village yawned, stretched and bobbed along sluggishly.

The trees in this village swayed gloomily, the petulant birds ceased their chirping, and the clouds made their way across the sky like slow, overfed worms.

The air held a tropical breeziness to it despite it being midwinter, and the river flowed along at a languid pace, gently teasing bits of floating ice to move farther down the stream.

As for the villagers, they went about their business half asleep with drooping eyes, sagging jaws and wide unconcealed yawns that spread through the streets passed on from man to man, woman to woman and child to monkey.

Lucy, too, had been affected by this strange lethargy that had enveloped the village. She was sitting inside the local inn, sipping a tepid cup of coffee, her head lolling to one side and her bottom tender from sitting on the hard wooden chair.

She was in a listless mood today. Everything around her seemed stagnant and dull. Often this sort of phlegmatic atmosphere is followed by a whirlwind of action, roaring chaos and deafening storms, or at least she hoped it did.

She needed a punch of excitement in her life and a swig of the old liveliness. She needed something to happen. *Anything*.

She would have fallen asleep considering the soporific environment but for the fact that her small pointed ears were currently being assaulted by the sounds coming from the corner where a deluded young man sat thumping away at a piano.

He was attempting to sing a horrifying rendition of the famous ballad called 'The Princess and Her Wandering Toe', and she wished he would cease at once.

She hoped the man would get a sudden urge to jump into his teacup and drown himself, or a tiny cloud would whizz in through the window, settle itself above the singer and proceed to rain on his head, instantly drenching him and giving him a powerful cold.

An angel, it seemed, had been passing over her head at that very moment, for her wish was granted and something did happen.

A sudden gust of chilly breeze swept through the village, nipping the yawns out of man, woman, child and monkey.

Lucy's head straightened, eyes brightened.

The sleepy indoor air shivered awake.

The river surged slamming the floating blocks of ice against the rocky bank until they splintered into a thousand pieces.

A cacophony of shouts, bellows and whoops erupted on the street drowning out the young singer's tremulous voice.

It sounded like the world was coming to an end outside the inn.

The old, dried-up man with a porous nose sitting next to Lucy's table stopped leering at her and instead peered out of the frosted windowpane that was letting in the dull grey evening light.

He stroked his thin white moustache worriedly.

Lucy followed his gaze and looked out of the small, low window. She spotted an assortment of booted feet racing over shiny cobbled stones.

A pair of big brown boots caught her eye, and she watched as it leapt into the air and click its heels together. Old green riding boots followed at a more reluctant pace.

Sweet feminine legs ending in slim, delicate leather boots trailed after large handsome ones, while tiny little childish boots were being chased by sensible motherly ones.

ANYA WYLDE

The language of these hurrying boots belonging to the villagers of Blackwell was mixed. Some were happy, some sad, some alarmed, while some excited. Lucy had never before realised that the lower part of the human anatomy could portray so many emotions.

Abandoning her cup of coffee, she tentatively moved closer to the window, a touch afraid of what she would find.

All she saw was whizzing booted feet

She stood for a moment curling and uncurling her fist around the dusty curtain of the inn in an attempt to warm her cold hands. The crusty old innkeeper had given her a table far from the crackling fire and, in spite of being indoors for over an hour, not an inch of her skin felt warm.

She debated joining the crowd outside to learn the reason for the chaos.

A wintery draft sneaked in through a crack in the window, numbing her poor cold ears and reminding her of the icy gust sweeping across the street.

She paused, undecided.

Behind her, what had begun as a soft murmur turned into panicked squeaks. Feet shuffled, skidded and crunched over the wooden floor strewn with peanut shells as people abandoned their dinners to join the swelling crowd outside.

The possibility of impending doom had put a spring in every step. Even the most lethargic creatures in the room became vivacious as they fled the inn with remarkable speed.

Lucy pressed her slightly upturned nose to the icy windowpane. The pounding footsteps, the clamour inside and outside the inn, and the spirited singer banging away on the untuned piano as if possessed by some otherworldly being made it impossible for her to hear a single coherent word or see anything other than chaos.

She slanted an annoyed look at the singer.

The young man did not notice her lethal stare but continued his assault on the piano trying to be heard over the noise. His fingers raced over the keys, his elbows joined in and at times so did his feet.

It was as if he wanted to make music with every part of his soul as well as every part of his body. He pounded the keys with an almost manic excitement, certain that this was the end of the world.

Soon his fingers, elbows, ears and toes were speeding over the keys faster and faster, striking darts of fear in the hearts of sensitive listeners. Finally, with a crash, his head hit the keys, and he lay unmoving.

And with the end of the ghastly song, Lucy became aware of the silence.

The noise had died away, leaving whispers in its wake.

The lane outside was quiet, with only a few stragglers rapidly walking towards the square.

She turned her head to find the inn empty apart from the gently snoring singer.

ANYA WYLDE

Plates of steaming food, ale, slices of bread and pastries lay abandoned on tables. A wine glass had been knocked over, the dark liquid snaking its way across the grooves in the wooden table. No one was around to clean it.

Even the owner seemed to have disappeared.

After a moment's hesitation, Lucy snatched the bread off her table, grabbed a chicken leg off an untouched plate and raced outside.

She caught up with the villagers easily and, pulling up the hood of her thin woollen coat, merged in with the crowd.

She moved along with the chattering bodies towards the square.

Speculation was rife in the air with some whispering about a fire, while the more positive ones hoped that the mad dash was for something more exciting . . . like free cheese being provided by the demented king.

Lucy stopped listening to the debate around her and started walking faster. The cold, wet mud had soaked her boots and seeped in through the cracks in the leather to dampen her stockings.

If she dawdled any longer, she was afraid her toes would freeze and fall off.

It wasn't long before she spotted the tall wooden spike that marked the centre of the village square.

Her heart started thundering in fear while her teeth furiously worked on the chicken leg as she joined the villagers, a dog, six cats, some sheep and a cow swarming towards the middle of the square.

She wondered what she was going to find.

Chapter 3

Time seemed to have paused, and a strange sort of enchantment had enveloped Blackwell village.

The grey clouds meandered over to partially cover the sun and dim the evening light faded to a blue-grey.

The mist crept out like a soft-footed thief and blanketed the moist ground.

Birds flew back to their nests, and insects burdened with their latest meal scurried home as fast as their many legs could carry them.

The night seemed to be lingering on the horizon, waiting to pounce and plunge the land into darkness.

The villagers huddled together in the square, having abandoned their shops and homes in haste. The lonesome village lay deserted with forgotten stew pots still simmering over roaring fires and burning tallows dripping precious wax.

All was quiet, but this time, the silence was not heavy with sleep but alert and tensed.

The temperature plummeted, and foggy tendrils began trickling out of hundreds of mouths. Men and women shuffled closer like a pack of newborn pups trying to get warm.

Lucy stared around in wonder, the chicken leg forgotten. What, she mused, had dragged a butcher with his knife still dripping blood, a laundrywoman with a forgotten pair of soapy yellow breeches draped on one shoulder, and a young man without the said pair of breeches out in this freezing weather?

"There," someone yelled.

"My breeches," the young man screeched.

"Ooh," the crowd gasped as they all raised their faces towards the sky.

Lucy squinted, her hand flying up to shade her eyes from the setting sun.

A few people started whispering prayers, and the old men became eerily quiet.

The children whimpered in fear and awe, while old women proclaimed that it was the second coming.

The young girls giggled nervously, one even boldly declaring that it was sorcery.

"It cannot be a bird," the old village doctor said using his dispassionate scientific mind.

"It has no wings," agreed the blacksmith, another logical fellow.

"An angel," a young boy breathed reverently.

"Hush!" His mother smacked him on the head.

"The Devil," a young girl offered this time.

She was ignored, though all those who heard her quickly crossed themselves.

Angel . . . . Devil . . . a wingless bird? All Lucy could see was a hazy dark blob in the sky, since her eyesight was poor. She stamped a small foot in frustration as she strained to give shape and form to it.

"Oh, it is dipping. It is going to fall," cried out a voice.

"Eeep," the crowd squealed, now bouncing on their toes in excitement.

"It's paused now . . . hovering in mid-air," the same voice commented.

Lucy scowled at the gasping villagers and impatiently scanned the sky wishing the thing would hurry up and move closer. She would race back to Rudhall, she promised herself, as soon as she had a clear picture of it . . . whatever it was.

Lady Sedley would be angry, but she had to stay. A few moments wouldn't make a difference. The speck was already larger and would be above them soon enough.

As if reading her mind, the contraption sped closer, and the crowd gasped, some in apprehension, while a few who now recognised it, in delight.

The flickering flame, the inflated white cloth and the woven basket could now be clearly discerned in the grey sky.

Lucy, too, made out its shape and grinned in pure joy. She had read about them in books, seen sketches, but to actually see one . . . it was breathtaking.

"It is a balloon," a few educated voices cried out suddenly.

"Certainly, a travelling balloon," a few more echoed in excitement.

"A balloon in Blackwell? Sorcery is more like it," screeched an irrational woman's voice.

"Foolishness," responded the younger men. "It is only a balloon," they echoed in superior tones. But in spite of the affected boredom, every set of eyes remained trained on the sky.

Lucy prayed for the sun to delay its setting for a moment longer. A few more heartbeats and it would be right above their hatted heads.

"It is descending," the children screamed running towards the rapidly lowering balloon.

The loving mothers rushed into action, grabbing their little hands and pulling them away from the balloon's landing spot lest they were squished under the wicker basket.

Lucy clasped a delicate hand to her stomach where a hundred butterflies seemed to be bursting out of their cocoons. The odd sensation was partly because she had eaten an extraordinary amount of iced lemon biscuits earlier, as well as the fact the balloon was rapidly speeding towards the ground.

ANYA WYLDE

She balanced herself on her tippy toes and focused her entire being on drinking up the sight.

Her eager eyes noted the dark silhouette of a man bravely leaning over the edge of the balloon.

The sun was now positioned right behind the balloon, and the fire burning behind the man, made her eyes water as she tried to see his features.

Black spots danced in front of her eyes, and her heart stood still.

"By Jove," someone yelled.

"By George," a feminine voice echoed.

"Egad," squealed the children.

The balloon was plunging towards the earth.

A hush fell in the square apart from the sound of a twittering bird and a cow chewing on a pair of yellow breeches.

The villagers waited in breathless silence, a prayer on every lip for the unknown traveller's safety.

Lucy feared the balloon would flip over in mid-air, tossing the fellow out of the basket, and he would fall to the ground like a wingless bird.

Nothing of the sort happened.

It was with an undramatic thud that the balloon rocked down to earth.

Lucy's heart started up again, this time racing in excitement.

The children screamed in delight, piercing the taut silence, and rushed towards the contraption.

The men and women swarmed closer on the pretext of caring for the children when, in fact, all eyes and ears were focused on the man before them.

Lucy felt the change in the crowd as they collectively took a small step back.

Shoulders tensed and mothers clutched their children to their breasts. The men straightened and thrust their chests out, while the old men gripped their walking sticks.

Some of the girls swooned.

A sense of distrust swept through the crowd.

Lucy, standing right at the back, was barely able to see the newcomer between all the teeming bodies. Her face fell as the church bell peeled.

She would be late, and Lady Sedley would not be happy.

But if she left, the question of the man on the balloon would haunt her forever.

A sharp intake of breath from a tall man standing a few feet in front of her as he spotted the traveler decided her, and she fell to her knees. She could bear the suspense no longer.

She *had* to see.

Accordingly, she began crawling towards the balloon unheeding of her dress.

She slipped between legs, saved her fingers from being trampled upon by boots and dodged excited children. The cold stones bit into her palms burning through her gloves.

She clenched her teeth and quickened her pace.

She reached the front and in a smile of victory gazed upon the golden-slippered feet of the traveler. The slippers were intricate in design with what looked like tiny rubies studded in triangular shapes all over.

Her gaze travelled upwards and encountered an emerald green velvet night robe edged with gold brocade draped over excellent shoulders and firmly tied at the waist. A dark handheld a glowing cigar between two long fingers, its smoke curling and flirting with the mist in the air.

Finally, her eyes fell on the face, and for the second time that day, she stopped breathing.

He was the most perfect specimen of a man. He had a long aristocratic nose, sensual lips, square jaw, sharp chin . . . and his dark eyes . . . his eyes were sheer poetry, framed by the longest, thickest lashes she had ever seen.

"Why is a hatless man wearing a night robe and house slippers flying over England in a balloon?" someone muttered.

"Mark my words," the blacksmith growled, "he is a loon."

The blacksmith's young wife shoved an elbow into her husband's ribs. "You are a loon." Her eyes turned dreamy. "I think he is wonderful."

"Wonderful," Lucy silently agreed.

ANYA WYLDE

"Lord Adair, welcome to Blackwell," the village doctor greeted the man excitedly.

"Lord Adair?" someone whispered.

The name floated from one ear to another, and within moments the crowd was beaming a warm welcome. The backs of men straightened, while a few more women swooned.

"Lord Adair, the Marquis of Lockwood," the children gushed in worship.

Lucy refused to believe it was indeed him; the famous, beloved of all England and legendary Lord Adair standing right before her common eyes. Her mouth dropped open in awe.

"Saved the king and the regent, he did," the Blacksmith said proudly.

Lord Adair looked over the edge of the basket and grimaced, no doubt wondering how to alight gracefully in a house robe.

"Oh my," the blacksmith's wife breathed, "what a lovely grimace."

"I apologise for my ungainly entry and my attire," Lord Adair told the doctor in a deep, rich voice. He jumped down to the ground.

The robe fluttered up, revealing his ankles. A gasp went through the crowd at the beauteous sight, and the women declared that the particular body part as perfection defined.

Lord Adair continued speaking as if unaware of the sensation his presence was causing. "My good friend Professor Bagwit recently procured this travelling balloon, and he arrived at my home very early this morning to show it to me. I couldn't contain my curiosity and bounced out of bed in my robes and directly went to inspect it."

"Naturally," the doctor replied.

"I was pottering about inspecting knobs and turning wheels inside the basket. The next thing I know a seagull is squawking in my ear and a cloud skims by my nose."

"Naturally, naturally," the doctor soothed.

"I looked over the edge and found myself miles above the ground. I spotted poor Professor Bagwit looking like a small imp, jumping up and down, no doubt shouting instructions on how to get down which, unfortunately, I could not hear."

"Oh, dear, dear." The doctor bobbed his head.

"It took me a good few hours to learn how to descend safely," Lord Adair finished, his black eyebrows coming together in an unhappy frown. (The village poet promptly swore to write an ode to those fine eyebrows while the blonde women decided to dye their own brows pitch black.)

"You must be cold," the doctor said.

"A touch," Lord Adair replied through blue lips. "If you have an inn—"

"If we have an inn!" the doctor exclaimed. "Blackwell has a splendid inn called the Pickled Boar. Blackwell also has a lot of wells, hence the name Blackwell," the doctor continued. "I must tell you about the remarkable soil we have here. Almost dark red in colour . . . so much water and yet not much grows here. Miserable place this . . . But happy to have you here. I hope you will have a pleasant stay. That is if you intend to stay . . . And if you do, then where will you stay . . . ?"

Lucy, still on all fours, ignored the nervous doctor's prattle. Instead, she focused on Lord Adair.

Even his back was handsome. She sighed and then stilled.

Lord Adair had stopped walking, and ever so slowly, he turned around to look at the balloon that sat in the middle of the square. His gaze shifted, moved downwards and fell on Lucy.

His eyes burned into hers as if taking apart bits of her soul and analysing it.

Everything around her faded, the sounds softened to nothing, and the world began to tilt.

The wet earth chose that moment to soak through her skirts and give her knee an icy pinch. She started awake and became aware of who she was and in whose eyes she was drowning. She smiled widely and blew him a kiss.

A flash of surprise crossed his face, and he quickly turned on his heels.

Lucy rested her chin on her hands and dreamily watched him walk away.

"Doxie," someone muttered above her head, and Lucy minded not one bit.

Chapter 4

With Lord Adair's departure, the sun decided it was time for a snooze, and the romance, excitement and golden warmth of the day faded away ushering back the dull practicalities of life.

All too soon the cold black wings of the night wrapped around Lucy and she shivered nervously.

The way back to Rudhall Manor was short but unlit and slippery with mud. If she wanted to reach the manor with all her bones intact, she would have to convince someone to take her back.

She finally decided to ask the old innkeeper to give her a ride in his cart.

It took her some time to convince the surly innkeeper and his equally sullen old donkey to leave the picturesque village with its cobbled streets and enter the dark, unfriendly road to the manor.

The journey was short, but the open cart and periodic gusts of chilly wind made it feel like hours.

Finally, Rudhall manor loomed up before them looking particularly grim. It had never been a pretty bit of architecture, but lit by moonlight, it seemed almost menacing squatting on the slight hill like an evil, warty toad.

Lucy leapt off the cart and raced indoors. Her fingers were freezing in frayed gloves, and the drenched, woollen bodice was dragging at her shoulders.

She sped down the hallway looking forward to a cup of hot sweet tea, dry clothes and a roaring fire.

Alas, it was not to be.

Hodgson, the butler, sympathetically informed her that she was to meet Lady Sedley in the morning room at once.

Reluctantly, she changed directions and arrived outside the morning room.

"The governess stole it."

Lucy's hand that had been about to open the door to the morning room froze, and her ear immediately plastered itself to the door.

They were talking about her, and it was only fitting that she eavesdrop.

"Why do you think the governess did it? Do you have any proof?"

Lucy frowned. That masculine voice . . . she had heard it before. It was a rumbly sort of sound. The sort of voice that made her feel odd in the pit of her stomach. And the words . . . they were uttered in crisp, cultured tones with a touch of melody to it. She shivered, and it was only partly because of the cold.

"She is the only one missing from the house."

That was Miss Elizabeth Sedley, the only daughter of Lord and Lady Sedley, speaking in her distinct throaty voice. Lucy shoved a finger in her ear and wriggled it about. At least it had sounded like Elizabeth's voice, but the tone . . .

"She left early this evening."

This time Lucy was certain that it was Elizabeth Sedley speaking. It was hard to mistake a voice that sounded like it was suffering from a perpetual cold.

What had thrown her off was the fact that Elizabeth was five feet, ten inches of beautifully sculpted ice. The woman never smiled, let alone simpered, but her current tone had held a certain coyness, a hint of womanly modesty and even a blob of dashed warmth.

It was decidedly odd.

"She has gone to the village." Peter Sedley's soft voice broke into Lucy's thoughts.

"She won't be back," Lady Sedley told her eldest son. "The day I set my eyes on Miss Trotter, I knew she was the wrong sort. We should have never hired her . . . I don't know why we did."

Lucy frowned and pinned her eye on a spider crawling up the wall.

"Who recommended her?" the stranger asked.

"Lady May. She is a good friend of the family, or rather was a good friend until she inflicted that girl upon us. She runs a few orphanages, and Miss Lucy Anne Trotter happened to grow up in one of them. Brooding Cranesbill, it is called. With a name like that . . . ." Elizabeth shook her head in disgust. "They did say she was well qualified for the task."

Lady Sedley moaned. "Alas, it was a rotten day when we took her up on her offer. Here we thought we were doing some poor unfortunate girl a good turn, and see where it landed us—in hot water, my lord, in very hot water. Would you like some tea?"

"Err, no, thank you. Why did you choose an orphan and not a relative in need?"

After a brief silence, Lady Sedley said, "We really couldn't think of any relative . . . ," she trailed off.

"They *are* your late sister's children," the man remarked.

"Yes, and with a fair bit of fortune," Lady Sedley replied with a hint of bitterness. "They are to get it once they come of age. We hired this girl, this Trotter, to teach the little monsters. Honestly, Tryphena should have allowed us to have access to the children's money. How she expected us to care for such evil little gremlins and pay for their education—"

"Mother," Elizabeth warned softly.

Lucy shifted momentarily, trying to get comfortable. She arched her back and rotated her neck and then stuck her ear back to the door.

She knew why they had hired her, a girl with no experience . . . because she had agreed to work for a mere pittance, and the Sedley family fortunes were not in the best of health at the moment. But they couldn't possibly admit such a thing to a stranger, who from the honeyed tones of Elizabeth and Lady Sedley seemed to be an important personage.

"She will be back soon," Peter repeated.

Lucy knew that Peter, the eldest child in the Sedley family, was currently blushing, for he always blushed whenever he uttered a full sentence.

She imagined his pale, almost translucent skin flushed pink, his eyes downcast and a few strands of fine blonde hair hanging over his broad forehead. He was an attractive fellow with a pleasant sort of temperament—a manly wallflower who seemed out of place among the rest of the Sedley family.

"Any other reason for believing Miss Trotter is responsible?" The stranger queried.

"Oh, so you are going to help us," Elizabeth exclaimed. "I am so glad Ian thought of you."

"I ran into him in the village. He had once done me a good turn, and now that I have a chance, I would like to repay him by helping his family."

"My youngest child . . . yes, Ian is the good one," Lady Sedley said, forgetting that her other children were sitting right next to her. "But I would not like to involve you in such a petty matter, my lord. I think we can find the thief ourselves—"

"This once, I disagree, Mamma," Elizabeth spoke over her mother. "I think Ian is right. We really should let him help us."

"It would be my pleasure," the man replied.

Lucy imagined Elizabeth nodding smugly as she said, "Now, let us quickly tell you all about this thief before she leaves the country and is lost forever."

Lady Sedley reluctantly picked up where her daughter had left off. "The governess's full name is Lucy Anne Trotter. Her parents were innkeepers, and they died in a fire or so we think. The details are a bit murky. Miss Trotter was five at the time. Thereafter, she was taken by a relative to the Brooding Cranesbill, which is an orphanage run by an admirable lady called Miss Marianne Summer."

Elizabeth made an annoyed sound. "Miss Trotter was said to be the sharpest of the lot, but truly it was a dreadful lie. The girl has been a nightmare. She has behaved suspiciously ever since her arrival."

Lucy relocated the spider and forced herself to follow its progress. It moved up the white wall like a drunken old man, scuttling up one way, pausing and then changing direction.

"She is always watching," Lady Sedley confirmed.

"She also likes sliding down bannisters. I caught her doing just that with the children the other day," Elizabeth said passionately. "How can someone who sings and dances with no one around, slides down bannisters and dares to call the master of the house an oozing pustule—"

"She did what?" the man interrupted.

"You heard that right. She called him an oozing pustule, and only because he pinched her bottom. Now, my lord, I would not like to speak of such things, being a lady, but she had no trouble yelling at the top of her lungs about her pinched bottom. She also threatened a whole lot of unseemly things when the other day poor sozzled Ian happened to fall into her room at a late hour. She could have been polite and shown him the door, but no, she punched him and gave him a bloody nose. My brother was pinked, my lord, pinked. Honestly, what sort of an educated lady does such things?"

"I caught her prying too . . . She likes looking at things," Lady Sedley added moodily. "She is curious."

"I don't understand what Father and Ian see in her. She has a gap between her teeth, an upturned nose and big brown eyes. She looks like a starved rabbit. Rotten thing, she is. Arrest her, sir, and throw her in the gallows. Send her to the continent," Elizabeth demanded.

"Hang her," Lady Sedley exploded.

A small silence ensued, laced with a lot of heavy breathing.

Meanwhile, Lucy wondered if the spider fell into a bottle of gin and was quickly fished out before it drowned, would it become maudlin?

Suddenly there was a crash, and then Lady Sedley's quivering voice said, "I am glad I won't have to see that vase again. One should not be forced to keep unsightly things . . . ."

"Just like Miss Trotter," Elizabeth finished.

Lady Sedley made a noise that sounded like agreement and continued. "It is a good thing her parents are dead or—"

Lucy saw red.

"Oh, you bloody rotten things," she screeched, charging into the room. Her entire body was shaking in rage. "How dare you accuse me of stealing? Rotten, am I? Let me tell you who is rotten, and as for being a lady, I saw you squeezing the valet—"

"Silence," Lady Sedley roared. "How dare you accuse me of such things? I have never squeezed anyone in my entire life. Pack your bags and depart this very moment."

"Oh, I will depart this very instant. Give me my salary, and I shall be out of this horrid place. I would rather go back to the orphanage than stay a moment longer in this pretentious house. "

"You will not get a penny," Lady Sedley screamed.

"Oh, yes, I will," Lucy yelled, charging towards Lady Sedley. "I am going to take every penny that you owe me, you rotten woman."

An iron hand clamped around her waist.

"Blasted, blithering fools, crusty scabs, toad-eaters," Lucy howled. Her hands clawed the air, and she squirmed to free herself. "Let me at her, let me at the frosty-faced witch."

"You dare call me a frosty-faced witch." Lady Sedley howled back. "Blooming idiot—"

"I bloom all right," Lucy broke in, "but I am not an idiot. You are."

"Why you miserable hag," Elizabeth moved forward a step.

Lucy struggled to free the hands gripping her waist. "Why look, Lady Sedley," she said sarcastically, "your own daughter agrees with me. I called you a witch, and she called you a hag—"

"You are the hag," Elizabeth said, jabbing a finger in Lucy's direction.

"Well, Miss Sedley, I know you are talking to your mother, but it seems you are now cockeyed. Your finger is pointing towards me instead of Lady Sedley—"

"I am going to break all her bones," Elizabeth screeched.

"Come and try." Lucy narrowed her eyes.

The hand at her waist tightened. "Stay still, Miss Trotter. Behave . . . Lady Sedley, sit down and, Elizabeth, put the poker back in the fireplace. Now, let us discuss this in a civilised manner."

Lucy took a deep breath, her hands were still trembling in anger, but something in the tone of the man holding her made her close her mouth.

"I am letting you go now, Miss Trotter. I trust you will behave?"

"I will," Lucy bit out.

"Lady Sedley, Miss Sedley, please sit down."

They went and rigidly sat on the pink sofa.

The hands slowly fell away from Lucy's waist, and the stranger finally stepped forward and into her view.

A familiar emerald green velvet robe edged with gold brocade gleamed in the firelight. The rubies in the slippers sparkled, while dark eyes peered at her from beneath long full lashes.

Chapter 5

"Lord Adair!" Lucy gasped in shock.

"You know me?" he asked in surprise.

"I saw you arrive in the balloon."

He winced.

"You did not like the balloon ride?"

"On the contrary, it was delightful."

"You looked very cold when you alighted."

"Currently it is you, Miss Trotter, who is shivering." He offered her an arm. "Come, sit down near the fire."

Lucy's lashes flickered. Lord Adair was treating her as if she were a lady. It was a novel experience after being seen as little better than a scullery maid by the Sedley family.

She eyed him suspiciously, but his bland expression left her feeling muddled.

She uncomfortably pulled the dress higher up her shoulder, suddenly aware of her dishevelled appearance and the screaming spectacle she had made of herself a moment before.

He ignored her discomfort and grasping her arm, nudged her towards a seat. He gently pushed her backwards until she collapsed back onto the overstuffed chair.

Her legs flew up, her wet petticoats slapped her ankles, and her back sank low into the large seat of the chair where her behind should have been.

She hurriedly straightened herself, and the raging anger in her bosom was replaced by embarrassment. She turned her face away from him, pretending to warm her frozen face in the heat from the fire.

"Lady Sedley, perhaps you can ask for some coffee for Miss Trotter?" Lord Adair requested.

Elizabeth discreetly pinched her mother's arm.

Lady Sedley reluctantly rang the bell.

While they waited for the coffee to arrive, Lord Adair began a gentle flow of polite conversation dealing with the weather, the state of the king's mental health and the latest cuts and styles of fashion that were sweeping across France.

Encouraged by the ebb and flow of his calm, refined voice, propriety dared to tiptoe back into the room.

The talk of lace, patterns and colours soothed heaving feminine bosoms. Further mention of shoes and reticules acted as a balm upon sore wounds.

Soon skirts were smoothed, snuff wiped away from upper lips, and adventurous locks tucked back into buns.

Lucy clasped her hands together. A large knot of unease had started forming in her stomach. She often flew into a rage and did things only to regret them a moment later.

She was regretting her outburst now.

If Lady Sedley truly threw her out of the house, she had nowhere to go. The orphanage had done all they could for her . . . To go back now as a failure . . . Her heart turned leaden.

The coffee arrived, and Lucy grasped the warm cup gratefully. A few sips of the bitter brew later, the tension in her shoulders reduced a touch.

"She stole them," Lady Sedley spoke suddenly. "Where are the jewels, girl?"

"It has to be her, Lord Adair. She is the only one who left the house and had the time to dispose of them," Elizabeth added.

"Ian was in the village, too," Lord Adair remarked.

Lady Sedley paled. Her eyes flew to Elizabeth.

"It wasn't Ian," Elizabeth said confidently. "He would not be so foolish as to steal the jewels and then ask you to find the thief. Besides," she added belatedly, "why should he steal from his own family? He could have asked for them."

Lucy snorted in disbelief, her quick temper once again getting the better of her, "He did ask for them just like all of you did. Lord Sedley refused to part with them. His precious treasures, he calls them."

"I told you she prowls and listens at doors," Lady Sedley snapped angrily.

"Peter, what do you think?" Lord Adair asked calmly.

The snuff box fell out of Peter's hand, and he stared at Lord Adair in surprise. His pet, a fat baboon, lounging on the back of his chair, scratched his head comically reflecting Peter's confusion.

"I don't know... Well, it could have been anyone."

Elizabeth snapped impatiently, "Oh, you won't get an answer out of him. He can't see beyond his frogs and rats. It has to be Lucy. She is the only one who went to the village after the theft. None of the servants have left the house since."

"How do you know what time the theft occurred?" Lord Adair asked, patting his pockets.

"We checked at half-past six this evening. The jewels were missing and so was Lucy," Lady Sedley said. A moment later, she asked impatiently, "My lord, did you hear me?"

"Hmm," he replied distractedly.

"Are you looking for something?" Elizabeth asked.

"It has to be here," Lord Adair muttered to himself.

Lucy recalled the words of the blacksmith in the village. 'Mark my words, he is a loon.'

Peter offered Lord Adair some snuff.

He shook his head, his hands continuing to dip into numerous hidden pockets in his thick velvet robe. He asked half-heartedly, "And before that, when was the last time you laid eyes on the jewels?"

Lady Sedley frowned. "The box was kept in a safe in the library, and I saw it yesterday at eight."

Lord Adair's hand paused in the act of upturning a lavender silk sock. He slowly raised his head and fixed a penetrating eye on Lady Sedley. "Therefore, anyone could have stolen it since eight last night. And I am sure a lot more people have left the house in the last twenty-four hours."

"But it has to be her . . . Who else—?"

Lord Adair politely but firmly cut her short. "What I am failing to understand is how all of you can be so concerned about the jewels."

"They were worth a fortune," Lady Sedley protested.

Lord Adair leaned back in his seat. He had finally found what he had been searching for, and he triumphantly pulled it out from his front pocket.

It was a glittering silver quizzing glass dangling from a long silver chain.

He placed it on his left eye and peered at every face in the room. "Yes, but surely Lord Sedley's death is more important? He was murdered today at five in the evening, was he not, Lady Sedley?"

Chapter 6

Silence reigned in the room after Lord Adair's announcement.

Elizabeth sat with her lips pursed as if sucking on a lemon, Lady Sedley appeared to be doing figures in her head while Peter sat like a calm cup of lukewarm tea.

Lord Adair rotated the quizzing glass in his hand over and over again, his face devoid of expression, while his eyes caught every nervous twitch, wriggle and squirm. His all-seeing gaze and the powerful magnetism oozing out of his every pore further added to the tension in the air.

Lucy's eyes slid away from Lord Adair's face and landed on the glinting quizzing glass orbiting around his long finger.

Countless women had posed on rooftops threatening to leap off and plunge to their deaths all for the sake of a kiss from Lord Adair.

A hundred-man army had once walked away simply because Lord Adair happened to stroll onto the scene.

Lucy did not think her common eyes deserved to look upon such perfection. Hence, she kept her gaze pinned on the spinning quizzing glass.

She wanted to forget her surroundings.

She wanted to pretend this was all a dream and that a moment from now she would wake up in her bed in the orphanage surrounded by a dozen babbling young girls.

It takes a man several years of meditating on a snow-capped mountain whilst unclothed to achieve the kind of single-minded focus that Lucy was trying to accomplish in a few moments.

Needless to say, it wasn't long before she failed hopelessly.

She failed to ignore the light of suspicion that was continuing to beam down on her. She failed to ignore Lord Adair dripping charm and sitting a mere foot away from her.

And most importantly, she failed to ignore the animals.

Animals that were Peter's pets, that should have ideally stuck to Peter, sniffed Peter and, finally, only cuddled Peter.

But this world is not ideal. This world likes to throw things at you that are the very opposite of ideal. And because that is the unfortunate truth, the animals did not do what they should but meandered over to poor, frightened Lucy.

Now, Lucy liked animals. She enjoyed looking at gulls soaring in the sky, ladybirds climbing up trellises or spotting a quivering little rabbit nose in a bush. But things became uncertain when animals that rightly belonged in the wild or with Peter decided to come and treat her as a part of the furnishings.

For instance, while everyone was wondering how Lord Adair knew that Lord Sedley had been stabbed six times in the chest at around five that evening, Lucy was frozen in place thinking about Peter's pet raven, Spinoza, who had perched atop her bonnet.

Over the last month or so, Spinoza had increasingly chosen her bonnet as his favourite daytime snoozing spot. She put it down to the fact that her brown bonnet, which had been pretty at some point in the past, was now akin to a nest with dried twigs, flowers and leaves.

But it wasn't just Spinoza's sharp beak a few inches above her nose that was bothering her. She was also concerned about Palmer.

Palmer happened to be Peter's favourite pet. Palmer also happened to be a baboon the size of a healthy child, with a long dark brown face, funny little tail and his crowning glory, the red, almost-mauve bottom whose sight always made her flush bright pink.

Palmer, the red-bottomed baboon, was known to approach people he disliked and slap them in the face. He did that to the butler once. Lucy had witnessed the whole thing. Hence, her wariness towards the animal who had currently abandoned Peter's neck to come and nuzzle hers.

But not all the animals that had popped over to her side were frightening. The two tiny pugs asleep on her lap were sweet, as was the gentle old dog of mixed breed that was helping thaw her frozen toes by stretching out his warm body over them.

She stuck her hands under the pug's bellies, and, now nicely warmed from top to toe, turned her attention towards the plate of dry sandwiches lying on the table.

"How did you know about Father?" Elizabeth finally spoke.

Lucy caught the tears in Elizabeth's voice. She wondered if it was genuine. Lord Sedley was not loved by anyone in the family, and as far as she knew, his death would benefit the family more than his living had.

Still, Lord Sedley had been Elizabeth's father, and however much Elizabeth resembled a frozen icicle in figure and personality, a tiny warm droplet must exist somewhere in the vicinity of her frozen heart.

"How did you know about the murder," Lady Sedley repeated her daughter's question with a hint of awe in her voice.

"Ian told you," Peter said shortly.

Lord Adair tapped the cigar. The grey ash fell on the fawn carpet. "He mentioned the theft that everyone is so concerned about but not the murder."

"You even knew the approximate time he was killed," Lady Sedley murmured in a hushed voice.

"How?" Elizabeth wondered aloud. "I met you at the door along with the butler. You have not had a chance to speak to anyone else but the three of us, and not once did we mention the fact." She fell silent. A hint of fear moved across her face.

Lady Sedley gripped the arm of her chair, "It has not even been three hours since the event." She took a long sniff of her vinaigrette. "Your abilities are magical. No wonder England sings your praises. I knew the moment you walked in, my lord, that there was something supernatural about you. All those stories of your exploits where you slew a hundred pirates and all those corsets you unlaced with a single piercing look. I confess, I doubted them, but now . . . I think I am going to swoon. It is too much . . . too much . . . ."

"Nothing of the sort. I met the doctor in the village. He told me," Lord Adair said, poking the fire with a piece of wood.

A nervous giggle escaped Lady Sedley.

"The doctor told you?" Elizabeth asked, a disbelieving note in her voice.

"He had invited me home. I happened to notice the Sedley family crest on the bottom of a handsome silver teapot from which his wife poured me a cup of tea. I remarked upon it, and he blurted out the truth. It seemed he, too, believes in my apparent magical abilities. Thus, I learned of the murder and the silver tea set he had been presented with to keep the whole thing quiet."

An uncomfortable silence fell after this. Lady Sedley busied herself with the knitting, while Elizabeth chose to stare into the crackling fire.

Lucy carefully sipped the coffee, trying not to disturb Spinoza, who had nodded off on top of her bonnet. She had been shocked at the news that Lord Sedley had died such a violent and sudden death, but she had seen so many of her friends die of want and disease while growing up in the orphanage that in some way her heart was well guarded and prepared for such things in life.

She peeked at Lady Sedley. What bothered her more was the calmness with which the family was treating the situation. To lose a husband or a father . . . She bit her lip and took a long gulp from the cup.

She almost choked on the coffee when Elizabeth suddenly leapt to her feet and pointed at Lucy. "She killed him. She killed him for the jewels. Father kept the key to the safe on a chain around his neck, and the only way anyone could have got it off him was by killing him. She killed him, took the jewels and gave it to her accomplice in the village."

"I did no such thing," Lucy roared, startling Spinoza, who squawked and flew away.

"Why did it take you hours to return to the house when the village is a mere ten-minute walk from here?" Lady Sedley snapped.

Lucy titled her chin up. "I went to the inn and after that watched the balloon descend. By the time I was ready to leave, it was too dark to walk back without a lamp, and it took me some time to cajole the innkeeper into bringing me here in his hay cart."

Elizabeth snorted.

"I am telling you the truth," Lucy said. "And besides, if I had murdered Lord Sedley and stolen the jewels, then why, pray tell, would I be sitting here like a blithering fool? I should be making my way across the country as we speak."

"What I would like to know," Lord Adair interrupted, "is why I wasn't told about the murder?"

Elizabeth quickly answered. "It is a family matter. We didn't want the whole village learning about the murder and then trying to steal souvenirs from the house. You know how it has become a fashion for people to steal and sell bits and pieces belonging to the victim. When Lady Herrington was murdered a few miles north, people were selling her toenails in our village. Lord Herrington had thieves sneaking into his home up until the funeral. Everything of hers was stolen from her soup bowl to her nose hair. She was finally buried wearing Lord Herrington's best coat and her sister's petticoat."

"We wanted to conduct the funeral in peace and then announce it to the world," Lady Sedley added.

"I am hardly likely to steal Lord Sedley's eyelashes," Lord Adair remarked.

Elizabeth's cup clattered loudly on the saucer, and Lady Sedley twisted the tassels of the cushion.

After a moment, Lady Sedley said, "We are grieving. It has all occurred so soon . . . ."

Lord Adair became silent, his eyes searching the faces in front him.

"The tears are on their way, are they?" he asked, raising an eyebrow. "Boarded the carriage, luggage and all."

"Eh?" Lady Sedley asked blankly.

"You don't appear to be grieving," he clarified.

Lady Sedley stroked her green dress, uncomfortably, "I am going to wear black . . . The maid is ironing the dress for me as we speak." She quickly turned to Lucy. "You, girl, pack your bags and leave my home right this minute."

Lucy narrowed her eyes, but before she could speak Lord Adair interrupted her.

"Miss Trotter is not going anywhere." He softened his voice. "Until we discover the murderer, we cannot let her leave—or anyone else for that matter."

"Truly, Lord Adair, this is a personal matter," Elizabeth started to say.

Lord Adair raised an eyebrow. "Wouldn't you like justice for your father?"

Elizabeth's lips tightened.

"Will you stay with us until the murderer is found?" Peter spoke up suddenly.

"I am sure he would prefer—"

"I would like that," Lord Adair said, cutting Elizabeth short. "Thank you. It would make the investigation easier."

After that, an uneasy silence did a short dance around the room.

Palmer, the baboon, started whacking a chair with a cushion.

Thump, thump, thump sounded in the air.

No one bothered stopping the animal's game.

Soon even the baboon gave up and went and curled on top of Peter's shoulder. He looked bored. That is the baboon looked bored, while Peter appeared to be asleep.

"Well," Lady Sedley said, trying to be an entertaining hostess. "Well, well."

"Yes, well," Elizabeth added just as dimly.

"Unusually cold," Lord Adair offered, "is it not?"

"Awfully cold," Lady Sedley bobbed her head.

"Bitterly cold," Elizabeth said at the same time.

"I should go feed the animals," Peter told the plate of dried sandwiches.

"You should." Lady Sedley pounced on the subject. "He has a lot of animals, a whole orangery full."

Lord Adair stubbed out his cigar on a cherished vase. "That reminds me. I hope my sudden arrival didn't disturb your dinner."

"Why no, what with all the excitement, our dinner has been delayed," Lady Sedley remarked.

Someone's stomach growled loudly in the room. Lucy feared it was her own.

Lord Adair waited politely.

"Would you like to join us for a late supper?" Elizabeth spoke over her mother.

"Please, I had a long journey. And I must tell you about the balloon my good friend professor Bagwit loaned me." He suddenly paused and looked directly at Lucy, "You will be joining us for the meal, won't you, Miss Trotter?"

"She prefers to eat in her room," Lady Sedley told him.

"I prefer no such thing," Lucy growled. "You have chosen to believe so since the day I arrived. Sent me a measly tray—"

"Enough," Lady Sedley snapped. "Lord Adair, don't believe a word the ungrateful wretch says. I am feeling faint at the wicked lies the girl is spouting."

"I am not lying," Lucy exclaimed.

"Please join us for dinner, Miss Trotter," Lord Adair said. "And please don't think of leaving this house until I say so."

Lucy nodded, trying not to look too grateful that she wasn't being turned out this night. She watched as Lady Sedley bounded up to Lord Adair and clutched his right arm. Elizabeth followed at a more sedate pace and placed her claws just above his left elbow, a finger discreetly caressing his silk robe.

Lord Adair, as if unaware of the two adoring females staring up at him, said in a bored voice, "I must send for my valet. I cannot spend a minute longer in this robe."

"Ian's robes might fit you, my lord. You are taller than him, but if you do not mind revealing your ankles . . . ?" Elizabeth suggested.

Lord Adair sighed. "Miss Sedley, I would wear a sheet fashioned into a toga if you allowed me. Anything but this robe. I have been wearing it for the last two days."

Lucy caught him wrinkling his nose at the emerald silk just before the three of them disappeared down the hallway.

She inched closer to the fire. She had not noticed Peter leaving the morning room with the animals and was surprised to find herself suddenly alone.

The sandwiches lay forgotten on the table. And the fire, which had roared in Lord Adair's presence, was now flickering half-heartedly.

The full impact of what had occurred suddenly hit her.

Lord Sedley had been murdered.

She felt pity, but not grief. As for the family's behaviour towards herself, she was not surprised by the vitriol. Lady Sedley had wanted her out of the house the very next day after her arrival, but Lord Sedley and Ian had insisted that she stay on. Lord Sedley had said that she was a sight for sore eyes and Ian had reasoned that they wouldn't be able to afford anyone else to teach the children.

The butler entered the room, distracting her from her gloomy thoughts.

Hodgson, the butler, was an old man who had been with the family the longest of all the servants. He was a kindly old thing who liked his drink and a bit of gossip. His puffy almost maroon face was expressive, and his eyes were small and wrinkled at the corners. He dawdled now in the room straightening things which did not need to be straightened in hopes of inducing Lucy to chat.

Lucy was only too willing to oblige him. Too many questions were bubbling inside her, and Hodgson was an excellent source of information.

"Lord Adair is a remarkable man, isn't he?" Lucy asked.

"Beloved of the king and the regent," Hodgson beamed.

"Beloved of the mistresses, too, or so I hear," Lucy nodded.

"A rare and dangerous thing that," Hodgson said, picking invisible lint off the cushion.

"Is it true that he can kill anyone and not be hanged?"

Hodgson smiled indulgently. "Not anyone, miss, only those who are a threat to the regent's safety."

"A threat to the regent," Lucy mused. "Well, he might as well kill anyone he likes, or rather dislikes, and then proclaim him a danger to the king or the regent. Who is to question him? The poor victim is hardly likely to rise from the grave to give his defence."

"He is a good man, miss," the butler soothed. "He was the finest spy during the war. Helped defeat the French. If hadn't been for him—"

"We would have still won," Lucy finished.

Hodgson pressed his lips together and remained silent. He moved on to wiping the dust-free lamp.

Lucy plucked a sandwich off the tray and nibbled the corner.

"He may not find the murderer," Hodgson comforted.

"You were listening at the door?"

"Naturally, I took your place as soon as you vacated it."

Lucy nodded. "As you should have."

"It is my duty to know all the goings-on." He looked back at her from the door. "Miss, I shouldn't be saying this, but you did a good thing by killing that fermented old man."

"I didn't kill him," Lucy protested.

The butler winked at her. "Sure you didn't, Miss Trotter, sure you didn't."

Chapter 7

Lucy perceptibly brightened as she looked down the long wooden table. She eyed the innumerable sweet and savoury dishes dotting the polished surface and dug her nails in her palm to prevent herself from catapulting onto the table and sinking her teeth into a warm pigeon pie.

She had grown up eating simple dishes in the orphanage, and ever since her arrival at Rudhall, the dinner tray sent up by the cook had been interesting but recognisable.

But here everything appeared to be exotic and colourful.

Near her own plate sat a bowl of something akin to eggs, except it had creamy yellow flesh with funny little brown spots all over. She gingerly sniffed a white lump which turned out be to be boiled fish and discreetly pushed away a strange soupy dish with blobs of green floating on top.

Finally, her eyes alighted on the only other dish placed close at hand. She wrinkled her nose in confusion and stuck her tongue between the gap in her front teeth. It looked like some sort of meat. Was it lamb drenched in gravy, she wondered?

"Sheep's brains in matelot sauce," Hodgson whispered, nodding towards the dish.

Lucy slowly put down the fork and leaned as far away from the table as possible.

Lady Sedley, Elizabeth, Peter and Lord Adair she noticed were sitting at the other end of the table. They were surrounded by piles of lush fruits, slices of bread, delectable-looking pies, pretty jellies, chicken, cold ham and cheeses.

She scowled in annoyance. It seemed the arrangement had been deliberate. She was surrounded by strange and tasteless food by design. Her stomach growled in hunger, and her heart bubbled in anger.

"Please ignore my pale complexion, my lord," Lady Sedley's voice floated towards Lucy. "I fear a touch of quinsy coming on."

Lucy rolled her eyes. Lady Sedley always felt something coming on. Last week she had complained continuously about consumption.

The week before that, it had been dropsy, and both the times the physician had patted her hand and told her that nothing whatsoever was the matter with her.

All she needed was a long walk and a drop of brandy.

Spinoza swooped into the room, startling Lucy into dropping her spoon. He flew in circles over her head, flapping his wings. He appeared to be searching for a good spot to land.

Lord Adair, unruffled by the bird's arrival, poked a slice of cheese. He turned to Lady Sedley and said, "It is unnaturally cold this winter. People with a delicate constitution are bound to suffer. It is unfortunate."

Lucy bent down to pick up the spoon, her attention only partly on the conversation. Her fingers touched the spoon while her eyes looked down the table. Her mouth fell open.

Peter's ankles were primly crossed, but he was wearing two different styles of boots, both a rich dark brown.

But that was expected. He often did that sort of thing.

What was unexpected was that farther down the table, Lady Sedley's pointed yellow leather shoe, trimmed with green silk and embroidered in pale pink, had hopped over to stroke Lord Adair's uncomfortable right thigh.

Lucy's eyes crossed and uncrossed themselves, and she slid a wary glance towards Elizabeth, who was placed opposite Lord Adair.

She found Elizabeth in a very queer position. The woman was not sitting but half lying on the chair. Her back was uncomfortably arched, her bottom was perched at the very edge of her seat, and her pointed toe, encased in a striped blue and cream stocking, had stretched across to make ever so tiny concentric circles on Lord Adair's worried left knee.

Above the table, Lady Sedley was saying in a perfectly normal voice, "I think I will write to the physician in the morning. My husband's death," Here she gave an artful sniff, "and the theft has left me feeling queer."

Lord Adair's right leg was now attempting to get away from Lady Sedley's shoe and nudge Elizabeth's big toe away at the same time. He replied in an equally steady tone, "I once had the pleasure of eating dinner at a friend's house. The duck had been lovely and tender that day. His wife told me much the same thing. She said she would call the physician in the morning, for she was feeling a little odd. She died that night."

"You don't say," Lady Sedley gasped. Her entire leg moved up his thigh to lie across his lap.

Lucy hiccupped at the sight and banged her head on the underside of the table. Her cheeks turned pink, and she sat back in her seat. She had forgotten the spoon on the floor. She hiccupped again and reached for the wine.

Lord Adair was now pulling out some sort of herb from inside a pocket in his robe and offering it to Lady Sedley. He was recounting its various benefits, but Lucy heard none of it. She was grasping the stem of her glass, her face turning redder and redder until it was almost maroon in embarrassment.

A loud hic escaped her lips, and all eyes swivelled towards her. Lucy hurriedly took another sip of her wine.

Lord Adair shot her a keen look before continuing where he had left off. "A brilliant herb saved the life of a man bitten by a cobra, or so the man who sold it to me said. I haven't tested it yet. I would be keen to know all your symptoms once you have consumed it."

"I suppose I am feeling a little better," Lady Sedley said hastily. "I don't think it is necessary—"

Lucy bit her lip and once again dived under the table on the pretext of picking up the spoon.

Things had progressed, it seemed. Peter's ankles were uncrossed, Lady Sedley's second leg had joined the first leg on Lord Adair's lap, and Elizabeth had abandoned the knee in an attempt to part his robe and reach his unclad calves.

Meanwhile, Lord Adair had dropped a hand over Lady Sedley's thighs and down to his legs, where he sat clutching the edges of his robes close together to keep out Elizabeth's adventurous feet.

With another hiccup, Lucy emerged back up. She smoothed her scandalised hair and held the cold wine glass to her warm cheeks. It was a good few moments before she turned her attention back to the conversation above the table.

"Lord Adair, the gooseberry cheese is wonderful. Do taste a bit," Elizabeth was saying.

A large basket of fruits blocked Lord Adair's view of Elizabeth. He bent sideways in an attempt to look at her. "Thank you. I particularly liked the apple stew."

Lucy nibbled on a piece of dry, stale bread. Elizabeth and her mother were leaving no stone unturned in their attempt to attract Lord Adair. No doubt such a lavish fair had been brought out for his sake.

As Lucy expected, Lord Adair and Elizabeth spent some time trying to have a conversation with each other by straining above the basket or bending sideways to look at each other.

After another few moments of weaving to and fro on the chair, Elizabeth burst out, "Oh, this is impossible. I am going to ask Hodgson to remove this basket—"

Lord Adair was out of his chair before Elizabeth had finished her sentence. "Allow me," he said and swept up the basket, walked down the table and planted it right in front of Lucy's face.

Lucy quivered from top to toe in excitement. If she had a tail, it would have started wagging madly at this point. She had hoped something of the sort would occur, tried to will it, in fact, but for it to actually happen—a whole basket of fruits within her grasp—Her fingers itched with suppressed emotion and a tear almost formed in one eye.

She had eaten a rare orange, stolen an apple at times, but here she was presented with so many different fruits that she had only before seen in watercolours. Her stomach roared, her eyes feasted, and with trembling fingers, she piled her plate with grapes, a peach, an apple and a few small plums.

She bit into the sweet, crisp flesh of the peach and tried not to moan aloud.

Once her stomach was somewhat full, she turned her attention back to the situation under the table.

This time she dropped a knife and ducked underneath.

A pup was lying on Peter's boring boots. She ignored him and swiftly turned her attention towards the more exciting part of the table.

Somehow, while she had been cooling her blushing cheeks on top, things had become complicated underneath.

Some mysterious process had confounded the feet of the two ladies present, and instead of sliding up and down Lord Adair's legs, their adventurous toes were playing blind man's buff with each other.

Lady Sedley's foot was caressing Elizabeth's calf in the mistaken belief that it was a part of Lord Adair's anatomy, and Elizabeth happily nudged Lady Sedley back also believing it to be Lord Adair's frisky toes.

As for Lord Adair, he sat with his legs crossed on top of the chair, the robe well tucked in with not a thread dangling over the edge of the seat.

Lucy picked up the spoon and the knife and once again sat up in her chair.

". . . died. How?" Elizabeth was saying.

Lucy listened for a moment, trying to get the gist of the topic.

The conversation had galloped ahead. They were now discussing Lord Sedley's murder.

She pushed away from her plate and leaned forward in her seat. The goings-on under the table was forgotten as things had just become interesting on top.

Chapter 8

"Odd," Lord Adair was saying.

Elizabeth leaned forward, her eyes intense, "The murder could have been done by my old Aunt Sedley. Believe me, my lord, no one else could have gone up those stairs without Mother's or Peter's knowledge."

"I see," Lord Adair said, taking a bite of his food. He chewed thoughtfully for a minute. "Miss Sedley, I don't think your aunt could have committed the crime."

"Why not?" Lady Sedley broke in. "She was an awful old thing. Bitter to the core and could never see anyone happy."

"*Was* an awful old thing," Lord Adair echoed Lady Sedley, "and since she was and no longer is, she couldn't have done it."

"Her ghost haunts this manor, my lord," Lady Sedley protested.

"Mother," Elizabeth said, lifting her palm, "Lord Adair is a rational man. After he learns the facts, he will be forced to admit that only a ghost could have committed the crime."

Lucy brightened — a ghost. Hah! This was brilliant. As long as she was no longer a suspect, she was willing to believe wholeheartedly in this ghost story.

Lady Sedley dabbed the corners of her mouth. "Lord Sedley's bedroom, where he was found, is two stories above the ground. The jewels were kept in the study hidden away in the priest hole. He always wore the key to the hole around his neck on a thin gold chain."

"The study and Father's room are next to each other," Elizabeth continued. "Only one flight of stairs leads to his room and the study. Not even the servants have hidden access to those rooms."

Lady Sedley leaned forward in her seat. "Now, at the base of the stairs that leads to his room is a small wooden gate. It is a unique thing fashioned to keep Peter's animals out. We were getting tired of waking up in the mornings to find all sorts of dogs and cats sitting on our beds staring at us. It makes one feel queer. One morning I was woken up by a parrot squawking 'morning' in my ear, and Lord Sedley found a tuft of cat hair in his mouth—"

"Mother," Elizabeth tsked impatiently.

"Right . . . Where was I?"

"The murder," Lucy prompted, now wholly engrossed in the conversation.

"Ah, yes," Lady Sedley continued, "the murder. Now, we had a small meal at three. I saw him next at half-past four, arguing with Miss Trotter in the garden. He stormed off to his room soon after, and that . . . that was the last time I set my eyes on him."

Lord Adair turned a direct gaze on Lucy. "What was the argument about?"

Lucy dropped her lashes and looked away. "He wanted," She paused to take a sip of the wine, her face scarlet in embarrassment, "to nibble my toes."

A brief silence later, Lord Adair leaned forward and asked, "And your reply."

"I said my toes were fat with sharp nails and I would shove them up his nostrils if he didn't mind his language."

"And pierce his thick skull," Lady Sedley said with reluctant admiration. "You added that in the end. I heard it all."

"I see." Lord Adair leaned back in his seat and stroked his chin thoughtfully. He gestured towards Lady Sedley. "Continue," he ordered.

Lady Sedley nodded and began where she had left off. "He had a habit of taking medicine for gout every afternoon. It made him drowsy, and he would sleep undisturbed until the valet woke him at six for dinner."

"We live in the country, my lord, but we like to keep London hours," Elizabeth clarified.

"Yes, it is fashionable, isn't it, to eat dinner past five," Lady Sedley remarked. "It took me some time getting used to it, but after all, one has to follow fashions of the day. I now ensure that we have our dinner no earlier than seven—"

"Mother, allow me to complete the story," Elizabeth said impatiently. "Father departed for his afternoon nap, and mother and Peter retired to the morning room. Now, this is the interesting bit. The door to the morning room was open, and both mother and Peter could see the wooden gate at the bottom of the stairs that keep the animals from venturing upstairs. That gate was closed. It even has a bell attached to it to warn Lord Sedley if anyone is coming up the stairs."

Lady Sedley's voice trembled. "My lord, the gate did not open. The bell did not ring. Peter and I heard nothing and saw no one go up those stairs after my husband."

Lucy felt her flesh creep at this pronouncement.

Elizabeth patted her mother's hand comfortingly. "Until the valet who found him dead at six in the evening. He immediately rushed down to alert us."

"You could have overlooked a servant going up the stairs. One often overlooks their presence," Lord Adair suggested.

Elizabeth cleared her throat," We are going through a few financial troubles. We don't have that many servants, and they were all downstairs and accounted for."

"The valet could have killed him," Lucy spoke up, receiving a glare from both Lady Sedley and Elizabeth.

"The physician said that from the time the valet found him, father had been dead for more than an hour," Peter suddenly spoke up.

"Which means he was stabbed almost immediately after lying down for his daily snooze," Lucy concluded.

"It was not a ghost," Lord Adair said firmly.

"How could anyone have killed him? How is it possible when no one went up the stairs leading to his rooms?" Lady Sedley asked passionately.

"A ladder outside his window? Anyone could have crept in and killed him," Lucy bravely offered.

"A bush lies right below his window. The ground is moist enough to leave footprints. The ground, the bush and the grass below his window were untouched. And surely someone would have seen the ladder. His room faces the front of the house, and the children were playing in the garden. They saw nothing," Elizabeth replied thoughtfully, for once speaking to Lucy without malice.

"Someone could have hidden near the room and waited until the deed was discovered and then wriggled out," Lucy mused further.

"Are you telling us how you murdered my husband? You seem adept at finding ways to kill people," Lady Sedley scowled.

Lucy closed her mouth and decided to try to remain invisible for as long as possible.

"What Lucy suggests is a possibility. In the chaos that followed after the discovery of the murder, the culprit could have escaped," Lord Adair said.

"It could be someone from outside? A robber?" Lady Sedley asked, hopefully.

Lord Adair shook his head. "Someone who knew the workings of the house well. It is someone in this house."

Lady Sedley, Elizabeth, Peter, and even the baboon turned to look at Lucy.

Lucy paled under the glare of four suspicious sets of eyes. Surely they hadn't abandoned the idea that a ghost had done it so soon.

She nervously swallowed a piece of orange complete with four shiny white pips.

Chapter 9

Lucy drained her wine glass and leaned back in her seat.

It was remarkable how a full stomach had given her a goodly dose of courage. It had uplifted her mood, and she hoped the same sort of pleasant contentment had washed over everyone else as well.

At the orphanage, the children had beamed after dining on bread and cheese. A quarter glass of milk and water had them burping luxuriously, while a sliver of the cake had them kissing their arch enemies in delight.

Here an entire meal fit for a poor king had not even begun to digest in aristocratic stomachs, and yet the faces around her looked discontent.

Lucy shook her head in wonderment. The Sedley family were a strange lot. Everyone apart from Lord Adair looked just as juiceless and bitter as they had done before they began the meal.

"Are you joining us, Miss Trotter? I think Miss Sedley proposed a game of loo," Lord Adair asked.

Lucy looked up, guiltily. She had been trying to stuff an orange into her reticule which was already swollen with bits of cake, bread and cheese.

Lady Sedley answered for her. "I think Miss Trotter would like to retire. The children wake early, and Miss Trotter is by their side from the moment they open their eyes."

Lucy smiled wanly. It was the children who bounced on her bed and tried to prise her lids open every morning. But this one time, she chose to oblige Lady Sedley and decided to retire early. She was feeling rather content after all the excellent food she had eaten.

"Do come and see the kittens in the morning, Miss Trotter. Bring the children," Peter said quietly as she passed by.

Lucy pretended not to hear him.

Peter had converted an old orangery at the back of the manor into an animal sanctuary. She liked animals well enough, but the stories the children told her about the kind of pets Peter had kept in the past made her dread the thought of stepping into what sounded like a tropical jungle where at any moment something large and fearsome would jump out at her and eat her up.

She muttered something intelligible in reply and quickly skated past him.

No one else noticed her bob a general goodnight and slip out of the room.

ANYA WYLDE

A single flickering candle burned on a small table casting meagre light on the staircase that led towards the kitchen.

It was in a thoughtful mood that she made her way down the winding wooden stairway. Her shadow loomed large on the wall, and she traced it as it walked. She wondered what Lady Sedley would do about the servants now that Lord Adair had decided to stay at Rudhall.

The servants were few for such a large mansion. Lucy often found herself fetching candles, warming pan and hot water from the kitchens instead of asking one of the servants to do it. She even carried water for her basin and assisted the scullery maid with carrying buckets when she had to bathe.

She grinned. It was a pickle for Lady Sedley. Lord Adair seemed like the kind of man who was used to luxury and would expect to find excellent service wherever he went.

She recalled his disdain for the beautiful green silk robe that he had worn.

A giggle escaped her.

If the robe had bothered him, then what would he think of the musty, flea-ridden mattress in the single functioning guest room? Lord Sedley had shut down most of the other rooms years ago to save costs, and due to lack of repairs, most of them were unusable.

How was Lady Sedley going to impress her esteemed guest?

She was so lost in her thoughts that she blinked in surprise to find the kitchen door before her.

She touched the thick wood fondly.

If upstairs she had received coldness, then here at least she was welcome.

Every evening after the children had been put to bed and the family finished their dinner, Lucy joined the servants for a cup of tea and a bit of gossip. It had become a sort of a calming, enjoyable ritual.

Today they would have a lot to talk to about—the balloon, Lord Adair, the theft and the murder!

With a thrill, she pushed open the kitchen door.

The cook paused briefly in the middle of stirring the stew. She was a stout woman with a stern, commanding face. She avoided Lucy's eyes and quickly picked up a candle and placed it on the table. She went back to ladling stew into bowls for the servants.

Rose, the kitchen maid, slammed a cup of tepid tea next to the candle. She did not shy away from Lucy's gaze but glared at her like an angry cyclops.

Lucy answered the glare with a placating smile.

It didn't work. If anything, it made Rose even more furious.

Lucy hurriedly sat down on the rickety chair and pulled the tea towards herself. She took a sip, careful to keep her face neutral. She wondered if she had interrupted an argument.

"Poor Lord Sedley," she said, hoping a bit of gossip would defuse the tension. "Terrible how he died."

Rose took a step towards her. The cook's hand shot out and stopped her. The cook ever so slightly shook her head while the scullery maid started scrubbing the floor more vigorously.

Suspicion was thick in the air.

"Is Lord Adair married?" Lucy tried again.

The handsome valet lounging near the backdoor replied curtly, "No, but it is rumoured that he was in love once. The girl was poisoned. It was the only time he failed to find a killer."

The serving girl made a sympathetic click with her tongue. Even the cook's hands slowed in their task as her ears strained towards the conversation.

Hodgson entered the room and joined Lucy at the table. He glared at the cook and the kitchen maid. "She hasn't done it, and even if she had, the old man deserved it," he announced. "Stop eyeing her like frightened rabbits."

The cook scowled. "You have reason to be cheerful. You will get a nice amount in the will to retire." She banged a bowl of stew in front of him, sending the contents splattering all over the table. "What will happen to us? Lady Sedley will sell this house and move to Bath. Who will hire us?"

"She shouldn't 'ave killed 'im," Rose said, eyeing Lucy with a mixture of fear and dislike.

"We don't know who has done it now, do we? We cannot be too careful," the valet drawled.

ANYA WYLDE

Hodgson pulled out a fine cigar and lit it. "They are saying upstairs that it is Aunt Sedley's ghost."

The valet choked on his ale.

Hodgson chuckled and turned to Lucy. "Do you recall that time you went to call Lady Sedley down for tea, and you found—"

The valet pushed open the backdoor. "I am not listening to this," he growled before storming out of the room.

Lucy blushed and nodded. She had found the valet in bed with Lady Sedley. It was the day Lady Sedley decided that she detested Lucy and since then tried her best to throw her out.

The butler grinned. "Yes, well, the ghost of Aunt Sedley appeared the day after our handsome valet friend was hired. It keeps the family from becoming too adventurous and trying to discover the source of all the mysterious moans and groans."

Lucy turned a brighter shade of red and dug her thumbnail into the cold candle wax making small indentations. She quickly changed the subject. "Shouldn't Lord Adair be addressed as Lord Lockwood seeing as how he is the Marquis of Lockwood?"

Hodgson's beady eyes almost disappeared as he squinted, trying to remember some long-forgotten memory. "I vaguely recall a scandal where his father had vanished some years ago. Lord Adair chooses to believe he is alive while the rest of England believes the elder Lockwood is dead. They treat him as they would a marquis but don't dare call him Lord Lockwood for fear of offending him."

"I see," Lucy said. "So he will not take the title until he is certain his father is dead. And his father has been gone for how many years?"

"Almost ten years, miss."

Lucy whistled. "So he is a loon."

"Aren't we all?" Hodgson asked philosophically.

Lucy shrugged. "I suppose." She drained her cup of tea and wiped the drop that had spilt on her chin. "Strange. I wouldn't have thought the ton would have stood for this sort of thing. I mean, how can they allow Lord Adair the luxury to choose when he takes the title? And what if he never does?"

Hodgson shrugged. "He is the only man in England not answerable to the ton. He makes his own rules, and most of the time, England follows him."

Lucy thoughtfully pressed a fingertip on a bit of dust on the table and flicked it away. "I heard he wore a different shoe on each foot once. It became all the rage that season."

Hodgson grinned. "I recall that summer. Men were hobbling all over England wearing one heeled boot on one foot and a flat shoe on the other."

"And when he announced that he liked the scent of roses . . . English, French and Spanish girls started dousing themselves with the oil of the said flower. It caused a shortage of roses for two whole seasons." Lucy smiled. She didn't add that she, too, had attempted to make the rose oil. Her efforts had been a disaster. The petals stolen from Mrs Bury's garden had rotted and created a dreadful stink instead of a beautifully perfumed oil.

Rose slammed the burned part of the bread in the middle of the table, putting an end to the pleasant conversation.

The butler sobered and said quietly, "They will most likely blame you, Miss Trotter." He jerked his chin at the cook's back. "The servants will stick up for each other, and the family will stand together. You are an outsider and have been here only three months. Apart from that, you have stumbled upon too many secrets. It was Lord Sedley who had insisted that you stay. He said he enjoyed looking at a pretty face, but when you thwarted his advances . . . ." The butler shook his head. "Be careful, my dear is all I can say."

"Lord Adair will uncover the truth," Lucy said weakly.

The butler eyed her silently, too soft-hearted to take her last hope away.

Lucy picked up the candle and, without waiting for the warming pan, departed for her room.

She crept into her cold bed and extracted a piece of cake from her reticule. It was in a sorry state but still delicious.

She bit into it and chewed thoughtfully. She had awakened that morning with a song on her lips and a bounce in her step.

Her life had been dull, plodding along like an old cow, but happy and peaceful.

She had prayed for excitement. She had wanted things to happen—the world to spin—and for her to float down the rushing tide of life.

"I am a fool, an idiot, a blasted nincompoop," Lucy growled whacking her head with a pillow, "wanting excitement, the world to spin . . . Stupid, stupid, stupid."

She was floating down a rushing tide all right just as she had desired, but instead of gliding down on her back while sunnily watching trees and birds go by, she was wet, cold and flopping about.

The river was tossing her up and down, the water creeping into her ears. She was splashing around trying to keep afloat. A passing fish was delightedly slapping her tired arms with its tail fin—

She blinked back to the present.

"Halfwit, halfwit, halfwit." She resumed beating her head against the pillow.

Everyone in the house was accusing her of crimes she had not committed. Lord Adair would stand by his kind, the servants would glue themselves together, and she would end up lurking alone in the corner trying to merge with the wallpaper.

They would recall her presence eventually when the time came to name the culprit.

She closed the reticule and put it away. She adjusted her head on the pillow and stared at the orange she had left for the scullery maid near the cold, empty grate.

She was alone, an outsider and dispensable. Hence, it was only natural that she would be blamed for the murder and the theft.

A hint of panic unfurled in her stomach.

She had to do something to save her bacon. She wouldn't let them lead her to the gallows passively.

She would fight, she told herself fiercely.

The next moment, she deflated. Her days of employment were numbered, and she had yet to be paid for her three months of work. If by some miracle she was saved from the gallows, then what? Where was she to go?

She sighed and turned on her side, trying to get warm.

The back of her hand fell on a smooth, hard surface.

She sat up and reached for the tinder box. The click-click of someone striking the tinder box always made her feel a touch uneasy. Still, she had learned to ignore her discomfort.

She lit the candle after only a brief hesitation.

A small parcel sat on her bed wrapped with a bit of twine.

She unwrapped it and found a crudely painted, round wooden blob-like thing. A small note accompanied it which said,

Dear Miss Trotter,

I hope you like the brooch that Pat and I made for you. I hope you had a good birthday. And I hope we can have a holiday tomorrow because you have drunk lots of wine today and have a headache when you wake up.

Love,

Miss Hepsy Gardiner

Nursery,

Second floor,

Rudhall Manor,

Blackwell.

Lucy clutched the wooden brooch to her heart. She had forgotten that it was her birthday. She closed her eyes and plunged headlong into a deep blue weedy pond of self-pity.

"Pathetic state of affairs," she muttered as she drifted off to sleep, "truly pathetic."

Chapter 10

Lucy had plucked all worries out of her bosom, before falling asleep, and kept them on the side table.

She let out a soft, gentle snore as her head slipped off the pillow, and her trim legs wrapped themselves around the warm quilt more comfortably. Her palm was tucked under a flushed pink cheek while her full lips had formed a sweet little pout.

The bed was larger than the tiny cot she had been used to at the orphanage. Hence, over the last three months, she had developed an admirable way of using up the extra space by emulating a greedy boneless cat sunning itself on a rooftop.

She would begin by laying down flat on her back, moving her feet thirty degrees to the right, and tilting her head approximately ten degrees and stretching all her limbs out as much as possible.

But as the moon climbed higher in the sky, her limbs would relax and contract around her just as they had done now.

She slept deeply and diagonally, confident that after such an eventful day, the dark night had brought peace for the moment.

Surely nothing more could go wrong.

The grandfather clock in the hallway struck three, and a chill snaked its way into Lucy's room and loomed large over her bed.

The pink in Lucy's cheeks faded slowly, turning white tinged with blue. The warm quilt covering her shoulders turned icy, making her shiver in her sleep and curl up into a foetal position.

Next, a breeze trickled into the room. A soft, gentle and eerie breeze that rustled the drapes hanging around the window.

The unlit wood in the fireplace turned colder.

Soon the quilt started sliding down her shoulders.

Lucy pulled it back up with a grumble and turned over.

The quilt once again wriggled out of her grip, scuttled down her body and pooled at her feet, where it sat like the present King of England, doing nothing whatsoever.

Next, it was the pillow's turn to behave oddly . . . It twitched . . . and then . . . it twitched again.

The twitching pillow acted as a flame, and the cold, eerie breeze became the moth as it abandoned the curtains. The breeze rushed towards the pillow, and the pillow twitched even harder.

They met near the centre of the large bed and leapt into each other's arms like two long lost lovers reuniting for the first time.

The breeze was overwhelmed with love, so much so that it decided to wriggle inside the pillow cover to be as close to the goose feather stuffing as possible.

The pillow shuddered and blushed, and the breeze giggled as it playfully began expanding and deflating inside the cover.

The feathery bit of the pillow twitched passionately while the covers rose up and fell down, rose up and fell down, rose up and fell down. . . .

"Wake up, Miss Trotter. This game is becoming boring."

The voice penetrated Lucy's sleepy ears, and she came awake. At once, she felt cold. She shivered and reached for the quilt.

"Ah, you are awake."

Lucy stilled.

"Your heart will now beat faster, your hair will stand on one end, and you must already be feeling the chill."

Lucy turned towards the voice. Her mouth fell open in horror, and her hair really did stand straight up.

Every single strand on her body was now facing the ceiling.

Standing before her was a tall, middle-aged woman illuminated by a fat beam of moonlight streaming in through the window. An old-fashioned cream and gold ball gown hung loosely from her bony shoulders while a towering powdered wig sprang majestically from her small, pointed head. Butterflies, ribbons and pearls adorned the wig, and a gold pin glittered on her corset.

Lucy gulped. The fact that a strange woman was in her room was odd, but what was odder still was the fact that the woman was shimmering and moving like a reflection in a gently rippling river. Her sharp, narrow features were awfully hard to focus on.

She was also hovering four feet above the ground.

"You won't be able to scream," the woman said, sitting down in mid-air and primly crossing her ankles, "because you are too frightened. You see, what you are feeling are the classic symptoms produced in a human being when in close vicinity of a ghost."

"Who ar-rre you?" Lucy stammered. She had decided she was dreaming. Only a dream could explain such things.

"Ah, so you can hear me. Wonderful. And as for who I am, didn't I just say you were feeling things that one feels when in the presence of a ghost? Girls can be so witless," she said eyeing Lucy like she was a rotten lemon.

"You are a ghost?" Lucy was feeling slightly braver. This was a curious sort of dream.

"Yes, I am a spirit, a ghost, once a human, and now a dead sort of thing," the woman replied as if this entire conversation was very dull and every moment was making her more and more impatient. "There is a debate, though, going on in the ghostly realm where women are demanding that females ghosts be honourably called ghostee, ghostie or ghosty . . . They sound the same but are spelt differently. You see the females in the human realm are often called girls, ladies, women . . . You get my drift?"

Lucy nodded.

"So, then, why are all ghosts called ghosts and all spirits known as simply spirits and not spirities or spiritoos and so on and so forth? Some female ghosts are pleased that everyone is treated equally in the afterlife, but some are uncomfortable with the sudden change."

Lucy nodded again. "What's it like being dead?" she asked and pulled the quilt farther up her shoulders.

The quilt slid back down.

She yanked it back up.

It slipped through her fingers and began shrinking away from her shoulders.

She gripped the edge firmly and held it near her neck.

The unruly quilt decided to recede from her toes this time. It climbed higher and higher until her legs were left bare and cold.

Annoyed, she forcefully tucked the quilt under her ankles and clutched the top bit with her fingers and held it still until the thick yellow cloth became exhausted and lay limp like any well-behaved quilt ideally should.

"It's like being alive except you can't breathe or eat," the ghost replied, taking off her wig and scratching her head.

"Why are you here?"

"Because I want to be."

"No, I mean here in my room."

"Oh." The ghost floated closer. Lucy shrank back. "I am glad you reminded me. Well, you see, I am offended. My feelings have been hurt as I have been unjustly accused of murdering Roo Roo. Why would I murder my own dear beloved brother? I need you to find the killer and prove my innocence—"

"Wait a moment," Lucy said. "Who is Roo Roo?"

"Why, Robert is Roo Roo. My brother." The ghost clucked impatiently. "Lord Robert Archibald Cuthbert Sedley, who died a few hours ago. I did implore him to haunt the castle with me, but he was always the adventurous sort." She chuckled fondly. "Wanted to see what else was on offer. The silly dear."

"You are Aunt Sedley?" Lucy asked, her eyes widening. "You really exist? You truly moan and groan at all hours of the night? It wasn't just a tale made up after the valet's arrival?"

"Don't be silly. I have been roaming these halls since my violent and tragic death ten years ago. I didn't feel the need to frighten anyone, but when that horrible Margaret started being naughty with the handsome valet, I thought it was time to appear and do what little I could to keep them apart."

Lucy flattened the frightened hair on her head and asked bravely, "You didn't kill him, did you?"

"Kill Roo Roo? I would rather off his wife," Aunt Sedley said miffed. She reached over and poked Lucy in the shoulder. The action terrified Lucy but didn't hurt her for the finger went right through her shoulder. "How am I supposed to kill anyone when I can't touch a single human being?"

Lucy shifted farther away from the fluttering ghost. "You moved the quilt."

"I didn't move the quilt. The quilt and the pillow moved on its own. It's in our constitution that no spirit may harm any human being, but a spirit may frighten to their heart's content."

"I see," Lucy said, looking confounded.

"After we are dead, to compensate for the fact that we cannot eat or drink ever again, we are given certain gifts. Our presence invokes all sorts of terrifying things. Whenever I walk into the room, drapes rustle, quilts and pillows act oddly, and sometimes the wind howls."

"Oh."

"Now, a man who loves his rum and has been forced to give it up because he has inconveniently died . . . well, for him, the urge to drink is strong even after death, and that is difficult. Very difficult. To compensate for his hardship, he is given some added benefits. He can produce orbs of light to distract himself from dreams of gin and rum or create trails of blood. The pictures some of these ghosts draw with the blood . . . sheer brilliance."

"So all ghosts are different," Lucy interrupted. Her eyes had started drooping, and she covered a yawn.

Aunt Sedley narrowed her eyes at the yawn. "I will return at another time for the report."

"Report?"

"Report on your progress. You do recall I asked you to investigate the murder for me . . . don't you?"

"Ah, yes." Lucy stifled another yawn.

"I am going now."

"Wait, why me," Lucy asked.

"Why you what?"

"Why did you choose me for the investigation?"

"Because you are the only one who can hear me."

"How did you know that I would be able to hear you?"

"I didn't know. I disturbed everyone in the manor, except Lord Adair, who looked simply too handsome to be woken and waited to see who would hear my voice. You did. You were the only one . . . so here we are."

"I see," Lucy said. After a moment, she noticed that the room had started warming again, and the quilt had turned hot under her hands. Her lids immediately felt heavy in the sudden heat, and she struggled to keep them open.

The vision of Aunt Sedley wavered and began disappearing from the edges.

When three-quarters of the ghost had vanished, Lucy yawned and waved goodbye.

"I will be back . . . back . . . back . . . ." Aunt Sedley's voice slowly faded away with an echo.

"What an odd dream," Lucy muttered, letting her head fall back on the pillow which had resumed its natural shape. Her small hand crept back under her cheek, the pink rushed back into her skin, and her eyes closed in blissful sleep.

Chapter 11

The morning sun cascaded in through the window.

Lucy blinked awake and stretched her hands, neck and toes leisurely.

The words 'The governess did it' bobbed in her mind's eye, and she froze mid-stretch as the memory of the previous day's events came careening back to her.

The budding smile withered and collapsed upon her lips, and her stomach twisted itself into a thousand colourful knots.

As if enjoying her misery, the sunlight brightened and raced into the room and proceeded to attack the small mirror lying on her dressing table.

The reflective surface made the light ricochet in joy, and a particularly sharp beam smacked Lucy in the eye and dragged her out of her gloomy thoughts.

She flung aside the sheets and frowned. The light streaming in through the window seemed different today. Was it brighter?

Her toes curled in protest as she padded barefoot on the cold stone floor towards the window and peeked out. It was as if a white carpet had unrolled while she had slept and covered the whole of Blackwell.

She breathed in sharply and flung open the window. It was still snowing, and with childish glee, she thrust her arm out, letting the tiny white flakes melt on her skin. Happiness surged through her.

If Blackwell could look pretty, then anything in the world was possible.

She felt as if the snow melting on her arm was seeping into her veins, restoring her good humour.

She lifted her chin vowing to fight with all her might.

They thought she had killed the old man, did they? She would prove them all wrong. Aunt Sedley in that strangely vivid dream had been right. She must investigate. . . .

"I told you she has gone daft."

Lucy yanked her hand back and turned to face the speaker.

A young boy of ten with a mop of shocking red hair stood eyeing her warily from the door. An angelic nine-year-old girl with the same red hair stood by his side.

"Pat, Hepsy," Lucy greeted in surprise.

The two children quickly stepped back, their expressions akin to a pair of frightened geese.

"Only someone daft would have killed him," Pat breathed into Hepsy's ear.

Hepsy cocked her head to the side, considering Lucy. "Batty," she finally agreed. "She was sticking her head out of the window in this weather."

"Wants to catch her death," Pat replied grimly.

Lucy slammed the window closed and turned back to the children. "My dears, I can hear you. I may be daft, but I am certainly not deaf."

Hepsy skittered back with a squeak. Pat bravely stood his ground.

They both regarded Lucy like she was a curiosity in the British Museum.

Pat finally broke the silence. "Will they take you away, Miss Trotter?"

At Lucy's raised eyebrow, he clarified. "People who punish murderers."

Lucy edged her way carefully around the room so as not to frighten the children and sat on her bed. "I did not kill him," she said, directing a bright open look at them.

"But if they do take you away," Pat insisted, "they will imprison you in a dark, cold place, won't they?"

Lucy nodded uncomfortably. "They shouldn't, but they might."

"That dark place will have rats that bite," Hepsy whispered.

Lucy tugged at the high neck of her nightgown. "Rats and mice," she agreed. She could feel the brightness in her dimming a little.

ANYA WYLDE

"Then they will take you to a place much like our square here and put a noose around your neck and tighten it," Pat continued.

A bead of sweat formed on Lucy's forehead.

"Will it hurt?" Hepsy asked.

Lucy gulped wondering how to change the topic. The two children seemed to be enjoying this morbid talk. They were eyeing her in fascination. "Would you like a present?" she desperately blurted out.

At once, tiny feet scuttled into the room. Prospective presents, Lucy noted, was an excellent way of banishing fears.

Two hopeful faces looked at her.

"A gift each in return for the beautiful brooch that you presented to me last night," She held out her hands, and they leapt back a foot. She dropped her hands but kept the smile. "I wanted to thank you. I loved your gift. It was thoughtful." She paused, her eyes narrowed to slits. "Does Lady Sedley know you are here?"

"No, she is still asleep," Pat said, sitting down at the end of her bed.

Lucy frowned. Surely Lady Sedley would not allow the children to visit her, not if she thought Lucy had killed her husband. She turned to Hepsy who was still standing a few feet away from her and gazing at her with wide, unblinking eyes. "Why are you staring at me, Miss Gardiner?"

"Will you kill us too, Miss Trotter?" Hepsy asked, more curious than frightened.

"Perhaps, Miss Gardiner," Lucy said sombrely.

Pat quickly scuttled off the bed.

Hepsy tilted her head and eyed her like a bird. "I didn't want to come, but Pat insisted. He said he wanted to take a good look at a murderer. We may never see one again."

Lucy felt a little hurt by that. One of the servants must have warned the children this morning. She kept her face neutral and said, "Would you like a souvenir from a murderess? You can show it to your children when you are older."

Pat grinned and snatched the old blue-ribbon dangling between Lucy's fingers. "I am not going to have any children."

Hepsy took the red ribbon from Lucy's other hand. "I will have ten of them. I can cut this up into tiny, tiny pieces and put it in decorative boxes for all of them."

"Would you like me to sign them for you?" Lucy asked.

Hepsy brightened. "Oooh, then I can show it to Rosy. She got a new doll from her father last week, but I wager she hasn't anything from a killer."

Lucy felt another pang in her heart. She wasn't particularly keen on the little monsters, but times like this reminded her of how they were orphans just like her. In a flash of abandon, she pulled out a second green ribbon and shoved it at Hepsy. "Here, keep this as well. Think of it as a gift this time . . . from your governess."

ANYA WYLDE

Hepsy clutched the ribbon to her chest, her eyes large. "We won't be able to see you again, Miss Trotter."

"We will sneak up here though," Pat objected, "and see her all the time."

"She will be hanging to her death soon," Hepsy said, shaking her head.

Pat's eyes brimmed, but before the tears could fall, Lucy pounced on him and started tickling him.

Hepsy forgot her fear and raced over to join in the fun.

***

Sometime later, when they had gone, Lucy leaned back on the single, hard-backed chair in the room and closed her eyes. Her heart was still beating rapidly from playing catch with the children. It took her a few moments of breathing slowly to calm herself and once again plunge into a world of grownups.

Things were looking grim.

She glanced towards the orange she had left at the grate for the scullery maid. It remained untouched, and after last evening, she wasn't surprised.

The servants had rolled together to form a tightly wound up ball of yarn. Oh, the butler may toss her a couple of affectionate words now and then, grateful that she had apparently knifed the old man, but he was no fool. He would never go out of his way to help her. He would remain loyal to the servants.

She shook her head in disgust.

It was fruitless trying to unravel the downstairs syndicate.

Now, upstairs was a different story. The Sedley family comprised of independent-minded creatures who were as indifferent to each other as a rooster is to a squirrel, unless, of course, the rooster decided to steal the squirrel's nuts or the squirrel the rooster's grain.

Nuts, grains and roosters, Lucy mused, distracted.

She was hungry.

Abandoning her meditations for a later time, she decided to go get some breakfast. After that, she promised herself, she would sit down in the library and form a decisive plan.

For breakfast, she was presented with two limp eggs, a bowl of unhappy porridge and no tea. Lucy squared her shoulders, picked up her fork, and like a soldier readying for battle who knows to take nourishment when they can, attacked the food.

It was a lonely meal, and she had no reason to linger considering the taste of it. Earthworms, she decided, would have tasted better sliding down her throat. With a shudder, she rose from the table and carried the plate back to the kitchen.

She retreated quickly from the kitchen. The way the servants had looked at her had given her a sudden insight into what the French must have felt when faced with a large English army during Waterloo.

She paused in the damp hallway, undecided as to where to go. Usually, she would be teaching the children in the nursery at this time, but now, with all the free time she had, she felt a little lost.

The library, she decided. It somehow felt like the right place to plan her next move. Accordingly, she headed down the hallway.

A glass cabinet displaying an array of stuffed dead animals distracted her momentarily. She paused to inspect what looked like a beaver in a bonnet when someone bumped into her.

"Pardon," Peter said. "I didn't see you."

"Clearly," Lucy snapped and then softened her tone, "I am sorry, it has been a—"

"Difficult two days," Peter finished for her.

She smiled wryly.

He did not return the smile. Instead, he swooped down to play with the two pugs who had come bounding behind him. A faint blush tinged his cheeks. Before he could straighten, Lucy joined him.

"You should name them," she said, giggling as one of the pugs caught hold of her sleeve between its teeth and tugged with all its might.

Peter reluctantly smiled and nodded as he gently extracted the pug from the cloth. "I am afraid you have a rip in your sleeve."

"One of many," Lucy started to say when a screech made her jump up in shock.

Peter, too, sprang up, his thin body tensing as he spotted the source of the screech.

Lucy followed his terrified gaze . . .

A vision of horror had manifested itself on top of the stairs. It appeared to be a creature whose soul was greatly agitated.

An unhappy soul enrobed in a glowing white robe that swirled about its feet.

It glared down upon them like a supreme demon staring at its supper of two biscuits and a baby teapot.

It had hair— lots of hair, sprouting in great masses from its conical shaped head.

Its eyes . . . oh, horror. The eyes were bright, red and moist looking. The dark shadows underneath these frightening orbs were deep and dark as a moonless night.

"The ghost of Aunt Sedley," Peter gasped.

"Your mother," Lucy corrected in disbelief. After a charged moment, she asked, "Did she have one too many last night?"

"It looks like she somersaulted into a pool of brandy," Peter whispered back.

"Undoubtedly," Lucy replied in shock.

Lady Sedley took a step down towards them. "Get the animals out of this house," she screamed.

Peter and Lucy shot a few feet into the air and sped backwards. A moment later, Peter said in a tone used for children or very, very old people, "It is cold outside, Mother."

"I don't care if it is freezing. Take them out of the house right this minute. I don't want to ever see them again."

"But it is freezing," Peter wheedled.

"I don't care a farthing you hideous, puss-filled mistake of my loins," Lady Sedley roared.

Lucy's eyebrows shot up to the ceiling. She had never considered Lady Sedley to be unreasonable. In fact, a few times she had caught her feeding the pugs under the tea table.

Peter wilted, his expression helpless.

"Perhaps you better do as she says. The death of her husband has propelled her into an abyss of despair. Lady Sedley, it now seems, is unhinged," Lucy whispered, watching Lady Sedley charge down the stairs looking wild-eyed.

"Unhinged? What like a door?"

"Yes, and you are the knob," Lucy snapped. "Hurry," she urged impatiently.

Peter grabbed the pups and hurtled towards the main door. Lucy, too, slipped into the library and shut the door.

She closed her eyes and rested her back against the door.

Her ears quivered, as she waited with bated breath until Lady Sedley's footsteps raced past.

She breathed a sigh of relief and opened her eyes.

Flames crackled in the fireplace.

ANYA WYLDE

She cast a look around. A smile tugged at the corners of her mouth.

She was all alone in a large warm room filled with the scent of hundreds of books, ink and leather.

This was perfect. She could now make her plan on how to trap the murderer in peace.

She sat down in front of the dark rosewood writing table and pulled a crisp, clean sheet of paper towards herself. Dipping a quill in ink, she began to write . . . .

Chapter 12

Lord Robert Archibald Sedley, Lucy recalled, had been a belligerent fellow. A rotten creature who had been bottle headed substantially cracked and had possessed a voice that seemed to emerge from deep within his intestines to break through his cruel lips in a bellowing, reverberating sound.

A sound that had shaken the very air surrounding him and had held enough power to send a weak-willed creature shooting a few feet into the air in absolute terror.

Along with his commanding voice, he had also possessed a lusty temperament, a lineage that could be traced back a hundred years, and blood so blue that one was amazed to see his red cheeks.

He also happened to have been four feet, eleven inches tall.

Lucy chewed the back of her quill, her finger tapping his name on the sheet before her. The ink was still wet and a blob formed where Archi had been. She did not notice but continued to drum the sheet with her fingertips.

Lord Sedley had, owing to his bottle head, squandered a good deal of the Sedley family wealth on what he termed as 'good investments'. They had turned out to be terrible investments.

His pennies would have been better spent buying rotten eggs or mud.

Perhaps it was his short stature, she mused, that had turned him into an evil little goblin.

He had been like a greedy little squirrel hoarding his nuts, refusing to let slip a single one into anyone else's hand, even if the hand had belonged to a member of his family.

She shook her head sadly. He wouldn't need those nuts anymore . . . .

She threw the quill down on the table and started pacing the room. Her hand absently skimmed over the dusty books lining the shelves. A layer of thick grey dust settled on her fingertips.

She sneezed.

Lady Sedley was a terrible wife. She was like that bird Lucy had read about once in a book; the beautiful bird who snuck her eggs into another bird's nest and then abandoned her unborn chicks to their fate.

Lady Sedley, with her mulligrubs, was also a swooner. An artistic swooner who swooned only in the presence of handsome men irrespective of their marital status. Her slim figure collapsed on-demand in a dignified heap and draped itself on the nearest fainting couch or chair, but never on the floor.

She had been ten years younger than Lord Sedley when they had married. They said she had been beautiful—still was, Lucy supposed— in an ethereal, incompetent and bleating sort of way.

Lucy returned to the desk and circled Lady Sedley's name.

Lady Sedley could have done it. After all, she had plenty of reasons to off the old dried up shrimp. She had despised her tight-fisted, stiff rumped oleaginous husband, and she was having an affair with the valet. His death now allowed her to sell this ugly manor and retire to the more sociable Bath and live the rest of her life in comfort.

Lucy's forehead creased as she recalled the cook telling her once that Ian had been thrown into debtor's prison some years ago. Lord Sedley had refused to help his son, and since that day Lady Sedley had eyed her husband with simmering, ill-concealed hatred.

Lucy slipped the list into a pocket of her skirt and went and stood in front of the fire. She held out her hands, letting the warmth soak into her skin. She wished she could store this heat somewhere and use it when she needed it again.

With a sigh, she once again dipped her fingers into her skirt pockets and extracted a tiny flask of brandy. After a sly look to the left and right to assure no one else was in the room with her, she took a swig of the contents.

The effect was immediate.

Warmth coursed through her limbs as the brandy slid down her throat.

"The blasted Sedley family," she muttered to herself. "May maggots fill their brains and poison ivy adhere to their behinds forever."

Family . . . Her heart clenched in pain, and she pushed away from the sudden longing like she had done countless times before and rapidly blinked her eyes.

This would not do. Her sudden gloomy mood, she convinced herself, was the library's fault. It was a depressing sort of room, and any mentally stable creature was bound to feel affected by its lonely weeping walls.

With a last finger waggle towards the sparking flames, she spun on her heels and headed towards the door. She stopped long enough to grab her thin woollen coat and stepped into the white winter landscape.

She breathed the crisp air scented with cow dung and horse manure in pleasure.

Dark, fluffy clouds rolled forth and efficiently covered the sky. An icy wind fresh from the north followed and wriggled a naughty finger down the back of her neck.

She pulled the coat closer around her neck.

The cold wind snickered and blew a powerful gust in her direction, making her lurch forward in alarm. It pushed her along until she had no choice but to go where the wind blew.

Spotting her favourite wooden bench a few feet away, she hurried over to it and sat down.

The wind changed direction and went to flirt with the Blackwell milkmaids instead.

Lucy wriggled about and got comfortable on the bench. She adored this particular spot for two reasons. Firstly, it faced Peter's animal house, which was an old orangery made up of grey stones, wood and partly coloured glass that twinkled enchantingly in the sunlight. And secondly, the sun, when it shone, warmed up the bench making it mighty comfortable to sit on.

She pulled out the folded piece of paper from her pocket and resumed brooding over the list of names.

Peter Sedley was second on her suspect list. He was the eldest, the heir and the one who would have gained the most from Lord Sedley's death.

Somehow Lucy could not see the shy, gentle and funny-smelling Peter lifting a snickersnee and stabbing Lord Sedley in the chest.

But human nature, she knew, was unpredictable and changeable. One day one may adore the taste of lemons and the next day despise the very sight of them. She doubted kittens grew to dislike the taste of milk or dogs turned up their wet noses when presented with a juicy bone simply because their taste buds had suddenly become refined.

An image of a sparkling white poodle narrowing its eyes at a plate of chicken in Robert Sauce flitted by in her mind's eye.

She frowned and forced her mind back on the matter at hand—the murder.

Who else could have done it?

Elizabeth and Ian. They both needed the money. Ian to fuel his gambling habit and Elizabeth for a season in London.

She shook her head in annoyance. Even the servants were none too fond of the master. Lord Sedley had been rude, often accosting the maids and lashing out at the butler. And the valet was having an affair with Lady Sedley. It could have been a crime of passion . . . .

Everyone, it seemed, had a reason to kill the vulgar old beast.

Lucy sprang up with a hiss of frustration. Her head was starting to pound.

She couldn't do this alone.

She needed help, at least in the beginning. She needed someone who would tell her the basic facts of the murder without sneering or growling at her.

A flash of red and black caught her eye. Squinting, she recognised the figure—Lord Adair.

This was her chance to ask him some questions. If he genuinely intended to find out the truth, then he wouldn't hesitate in guiding her in the right direction.

She steeled her fluttering stomach, and before she could lose her nerve made her way towards him.

Chapter 13

She stood a few feet away from him, watching his back.

And, oh, what a back it was.

A giant golden dragon was woven into the black fabric of his robe. The shimmering fire emanating from the dragon's mouth seemed to caress his broad shoulders.

An icy gust of wind sent the velvet cloth rippling like a dark, disturbed pond. The robe, she noted, was too long for him. It pooled at his feet, stark against the snow-covered ground.

She wondered at her own courage. She was still amazed at the bold manner in which she had addressed him that day in the morning room. She felt a bit like a hero in a fairy tale who plunged into danger in spite of trembling like a leaf inside.

And here she was once again skirting the edges of danger; daring to speak to Lord William Ellsworth Hartell Adair, the Marquis of Lockwood, beloved of the king, the regent and the mistresses. Feared by all of France and England, whose exploits—

"It is ghastly."

Lucy jumped in shock.

He had turned towards her, his dark pupils flashing below sleepy lids.

Her eyes unglazed, and she hastily curtsied.

"Do you agree?" he prompted.

"Agree?" she asked befuddled.

"This," he gestured towards his robe.

Lucy eyed the red fur lovingly sewn onto the collar of the robe hanging like two long fox tails down his front. He looked, she thought dreamily, like a powerful wizard from some magical land. Even the air around him felt charged with suppressed energy.

"Well?" he asked impatiently.

Lucy detached her tongue from the roof of her mouth. "It looks . . . You look bang-up, my lord."

"It sheds," he said sourly shaking the furry tails.

Lucy nodded sympathetically. "And it's a robe again. I understand, my lord."

"You do?"

"I do. A robe with an opening down the centre. Awfully inconvenient when all sorts of feet want to creep in." Her eyes widened in shock as she replayed that sentence in her head.

"Miss Trotter!"

"I am sorry," Lucy gasped. "I thought you might be tired of wearing robes and wanting breeches once again. Blast it! I mean to say or rather I didn't mean to say breeches." Here she clutched her throat and hacked a few times in an attempt to strangle her throat and arrest the words in her tonsil, but it didn't work. "Surely," the words wheezed out of her, "it is better to talk of breeches than robes with openings for feet to slip in." She finished by slapping a horrified hand to her mouth.

"Miss—"

"I know, I know," she babbled in dismay, "I am sorry. So, so sorry. I apologise profusely, my lord. You see, I was trying to explain what I meant, but I happened to repeat the fact that I said robes with—"

He placed a finger on her lips, immediately silencing her.

She gulped and pressed her lips together.

"Miss Trotter," he said sternly, "you are supposed to be an educated young lady. Kindly behave like one."

She hurriedly bobbed her head.

"And your bonnet is frightful." He adjusted the offending thing so that it tilted at a more flattering angle. "If you have to wear it, wear it thus."

"But I can no longer see from one eye," she protested. "The brim is covering it."

"Suffer, my dear, for the sake of fashion," he ordered.

Lucy reluctantly nodded again and pinned her eye on the frozen stream next to his foot.

"It belongs to Miss Sedley's uncle," he remarked, once again gesturing towards the robe. "He must have been a giant," he went on, pulling up the sleeves that kept sliding forward to engulf his whole hand.

She made an indistinct noise in her throat.

His lips quirked in amusement. "I suppose I shouldn't be complaining about a perfectly warm robe when you are rapidly turning into an ice sculpture." He stopped abruptly and turned back to stare out into the distance, the smile still lingering on his lips.

Lucy pulled the coat tighter across her shoulders and followed Lord Adair's gaze.

She stilled.

Lord Adair slanted a look at her. His voice was wary when he asked, "What, pray tell, is that, Miss Trotter?"

Lucy ever so slowly moved a few steps behind Lord Adair. "She is called Spooner, my lord."

"I see, and what manner of creature is it?"

"It is a bird," she replied from the corner of her mouth.

"What sort?"

"It is, I believe, an Egyptian crane."

"Why is it in England?"

"Peter brought her over from Africa."

"I like birds, Miss Trotter. In fact, I could be considered a bird lover, but that creature has a nasty glint in her eye."

"I have never trusted Spooner, my lord. And I would advise you not to either."

They stood shivering in the cold, watching the bird from the corner of their eyes.

"Someone should explain the process of migration to Spooner. Warmer climates may improve her temperament," Lucy said through cold lips.

"Miss Trotter," Lord Adair said, turning to face her, "what do you want?"

Her eyes widened. "How do you know I want anything?"

"You are standing here in inch deep snow, your inadequate boots soaking wet, your lips turning blue, glaring at an Egyptian bird instead of sitting indoors with a warm cup of tea."

"Ah, yes," she said and with another nervous glance at Spooner quickly came to the point. "How did Lord Sedley die?"

"He was stabbed three times with a small knife in the middle of his chest," he replied promptly.

"I would like to know all the facts please."

"The murder occurred at around five in the evening and was discovered at six by the valet. You were the last person to see him at around four-thirty in the garden when you had an argument with him."

"Did he fight the killer?"

"He had a habit of taking a drug in the afternoon for gout, which made him drowsy. Thereafter, he would take a short nap and wake up at six, get ready and come down for dinner. Whoever killed him waited until the medicine had its effect, and he was in a deep sleep."

"Hmm," Lucy said, sticking her tongue between the gap in her front teeth. "The key to the safe was always on a chain around his neck. Someone killed him, took the key and the stole the jewels."

Lord Adair remained silent.

"Where was the key found?" she asked.

His dark eyes blazed briefly. "It was still around Lord Sedley's neck when the valet found him."

Lucy stamped her foot partly to warm them and partly in frustration. "Why would he or she murder Lord Sedley for the key, steal the jewels and then take the risk of hanging the key back around his neck?"

"We should return indoors," Lord Adair said instead of answering her question.

He offered her his arm.

"Unless the thief did not want anyone to know he is the thief. I mean, he did not want anyone to connect the theft with the murder," Lucy mused ignoring his arm.

"I will find the person responsible, Miss Trotter. Have faith."

"In what?"

"If you are innocent, you will not be punished."

"I lost my family and spent most of my life in an orphanage. I was punished for no fault of mine. Why would things change now?"

"That was an unfortunate incident. This is a murder which is being investigated. We are actively searching for the truth."

"You will protect your own kind, my lord. I am the outsider," Lucy said, entering the house and yanking off her drenched woollen gloves. "I don't blame you. I would protect my friends too."

"Miss Trotter," Lord Adair said gently, "You are wrong. I will stand by the truth, even if it means sending my closest friend to the gallows."

"Lofty words," Lucy muttered under her breath. Aloud, she said, "No harm in me nosing about as well. After all, it is my neck that is dangling near the noose. Desperation may help me solve the case quicker than you, my lord."

"Or blind you," he replied, amused. "My advice to you is to stay in your room until the culprit is found . . . but I have a feeling you are going to be contrary. People are predictable, Miss Trotter."

Lucy dropped her parasol on his foot. Her eyes flared in satisfaction seeing the knowing smile wiped off his face. "Not so predictable am I, my lord, or you would have saved you poor toe just now."

He grinned in appreciation. "It is a wager, Miss Trotter. Let us see who finds the culprit first."

He held out his hand, and after eyeing his masculine fingers encased in an expensive leather glove for a moment, she grasped it firmly and shook it. "It is a wager, Lord Adair."

She unpeeled her coat. "What does the winner get?"

"Anything you fancy," he murmured with a glint in his eye.

"Agreed," she said promptly. "What I want, my lord is employment. If I win, then you will have to hire me to work as your assistant."

Lord Adair paled. "Well, now, I don't need an assistant."

"A housekeeper?"

"No, now see here—"

"If you have any illegitimate children, then their governess—"

"Miss Trotter," he scolded, "anything you fancy was the wrong thing to say . . . I meant—"

"Scullery maid?" she asked in a small voice. "Surely you need a scullery maid. You must have so many rooms."

"I have no rooms. I live under the stars," Lord Adair snapped.

"Ground sweeper?"

"Eh?"

"Surely you need someone to sweep the ground before you lie down on it to sleep."

ANYA WYLDE

Lord Adair opened his mouth and closed it again. He shook his head, and without another word, walked away.

A mischievous smile spread over Lucy's face. He was delightfully easy to tease.

He stopped before turning the corner and looked back at her.

Lucy's heart started racing, and her palms turned sweaty.

His departing expression was confusing, complicated and intensely beautiful.

She gulped.

He sent her a parting grin before vanishing from her sight.

She gasped and clutched the nearby hat-stand for support and held on for dear life since her knees had decided to follow Lord Adair, leaving the rest of her wobbling and unbalanced.

She sighed.

It was awfully hard to argue with handsome men, and Lord Adair happened to be the most handsome of the lot.

ANYA WYLDE

Chapter 14

Someone had let it slip that Lord Sedley was dead. The fact was no longer a secret, and the funeral was in a few hours.

Lucy sat at the small desk in her room, watching the visitors come and go. The snow outside had been churned by numerous feet belonging to the villagers and relatives, and the beautiful sparkling white ground of the morning had turned into a slush of brown and grey.

She was surprised that so many people had managed to make their way to the house considering the dark, roiling sky. A storm was threatening to arrive at any moment. The leaves had stilled, the wind had fallen silent, and the sun cowered somewhere behind dense clouds.

"Boo!"

"Pat," Lucy squeaked, her hand on her thundering heart, "you frightened me."

"I meant to," he said, strolling into the room. He peeked out of the window and made a face as he watched a woman with peacock feathers in a broad-brimmed hat alight from a carriage. "That one," he said grimly, "tried to detach my cheeks from my face."

An old man shuffled after the woman, his back almost bent double, and a walking stick clutched in his shaking hand.

"And him," He shook his head in disgust, "he coos."

Lucy bit back a smile. "You shouldn't be here."

He nodded. "We know."

Hepsy came and stood on the other side of Lucy's chair. "We were told to stay away from you, or we wouldn't be given any pudding."

Pat thumped Lucy's back in a brotherly fashion. "But we wanted to come and see you."

"Your pudding," Lucy tried weakly.

"We stole some already and hid it," Hepsy soothed.

Lucy turned back to the window, her chin coming to rest on her hands.

"What is a wig-eel?" Hepsy asked, copying Lucy's stance.

"Not wig-eel," Pat chortled. "Vigil. Lord Adair's valet arrived last night. Hepsy asked him to tea in the nursery with the dolls, and he said he couldn't on account of his having to keep a vigil."

Lucy's brow cleared. "He must have kept a vigil along with another person in Lord Sedley's room last night."

"To keep away the thieves," Pat remarked with a superior sniff.

Lucy shook her head. "Let me tell you a true story. It will explain why one needs to keep a vigil over a dead body."

Pat and Hepsy nodded eagerly.

Lucy's lips quirked. "A few years ago an ancient cook in the orphanage died, and up until the funeral, two people were constantly in the room with the body keeping vigil."

"Why?" Hepsy asked.

"That is exactly what I wondered, too, Miss Gardiner. Why did they sit with a corpse? Were they not frightened of ghosts and things? Or were they simply a morbid lot?"

"And then?" Hepsy prompted.

"Well, on the day of the funeral—"

"Yes, yes." Hepsy straightened up.

"Let her finish," Pat growled impatiently.

Hepsy subsided.

"And then," Lucy continued, "on the day of the funeral the dead cook's cheerful husband went to close the coffin so that he could carry it to the burial site, when suddenly—" Here Lucy paused.

"What? Oh, do tell, Miss Trotter," Hepsy begged, and this time even Pat leaned forward.

"When suddenly the old dead cook sprang into sitting position and demanded a bottle of gin, two pieces of fish and a cup of flour."

"But she was dead," gasped Pat.

"Ooh," Hepsy exclaimed at the same time.

"Physicians are known to make mistakes. She was still alive when I left the orphanage."

"So a vigil is kept," Pat said, his eyes wide in understanding, "in case the dead are not really dead."

Lucy nodded broodingly. She hoped that this time, too, Lord Sedley would bounce out of the coffin and ask to pinch a maid's bottom. All her worries would melt away, and she would even kiss the lusty old man in relief.

But nothing of the sort occurred. Lucy watched the coffin leave the house, and when the family came back, Lord Sedley did not accompany them.

Lucy and the children watched the rest of the guests return wearing all black and heads bent low. It was as if a string had been attached to their chins and someone invisible on the ground held the other end and pulled with all their might.

Pat sighed loudly. "I wonder how long it will take the worms to eat him up until only the bones are left."

"You should return to the nursery," Lucy said, pushing away from the desk. She stood up and stretched. After a moment, she looked down to find the children eyeing her queerly. "What is it?"

"We are going to uncle Dolton's house for a few weeks," Pat said, staring at his boots.

"We may not see you again," Hepsy added.

"I am here for a month at least," Lucy lied. "You will see me when you return."

The faces brightened.

"Now, hurry back to the nursery, you must have a lot to pack," she continued in a high, cheerful voice.

The children nodded, and before they knew what was happening, Lucy had ushered them outside, given them two sound kisses, a tight hug and sent them on their way in a much-improved temperament.

Lucy watched them leave with mixed feelings. A part of her was sad. She had become fond of them, but mostly she was pleased that the monsters would be out of her way and leave her to investigate in peace.

The children may have become sentimental thinking she was going to die, but Lucy had not forgotten the horrifying antics they were capable of.

She recalled the time they had slathered a sticky paste of flour and water all over her hair while she slept. It had taken her three whole hours to clean the muck out of her hair. Her arms had been aching dreadfully by the time she had finished.

Shuddering at the memory, she banged the door closed in relief.

***

Lucy surveyed the contents of her cupboard. Three-morning dresses, which were meant to be white but were now grey with age, lay folded neatly on a shelf.

Two faded evening dresses, one of which had tiny eyelets all over and often frightened her half to death, sat next to the morning ones.

Finally, right at the bottom under her chemises, she found a well patched, thick woollen dress in a wonderful colour of dirt. She pulled it out and laid it on the bed.

She cocked her head to the side and fingered the rough material.

It would do.

Next, she pulled open the drawers in the small desk in her room, her mind busy while her hands worked.

She had been the last person to see Lord Sedley alive, she thought, as she searched through the drawer's contents. And not only had she seen the hideous blob, but she had gone on to have a full-blown argument with him in front of witnesses.

She paused to inspect the yellow yarn she found in the bottom drawer. She flung it back with an impatient shake and continued her search as well as the line of thought. She had arrived a mere three months ago, and in such a short time it was impossible to expect she had formed an everlasting bond with anyone in the manor. Her position as a governess ensured that she belonged neither with the servants nor the family.

She stood up, clutching a pair of scissors and some green thread. She placed it next to the dress.

It suited everyone in Rudhall to have her proclaimed the culprit. She dragged a shawl out of the cupboard and flung it about her shoulders.

A thrill went through her small, slim form.

She was not going to let them win. She, Miss Lucy Anne Trotter, was going to unmask the criminal.

Her chin jerked up, and her eyes flashed.

She strode out of the door and down the stairs. She was no longer going to sit and think and muse and mull.

It was time for action. She had a plan.

An excellent plan.

Rose sauntered by carrying an armload of laundry. She paused long enough to send Lucy a superior look.

Lucy smiled philosophically. Ah, the silly maid would learn the truth soon enough. She chose to forgive the poor mortal creature, for the maid knew not what she was doing. She was blowing raspberries at Lucy—the great Lucy Anne Trotter—who would go down in history as the greatest investigator ever known to mankind.

The very same Lucy Anne Trotter who would soon unmask the killer and present him or her on a gilded platter to Lord Adair. Oh, the foolish maid would be sorry then. So, so sorry.

Rose narrowed her eyes.

Lucy sniffed smugly, raised her nose in the air and then promptly tripped over her feet.

ANYA WYLDE

She lay face down like an egg dropped from a height and spread all over the floor.

A giggle somewhere behind her made her scramble back up. Her face was bright red as she scuttled towards the door.

Her ego was bruised, but her heart was no less determined.

***

An hour later, Lucy peeped into the morning room from the corner of the French window.

No one was around.

She clutched the bundle she was holding close to her chest with one hand and opened the window with the other.

Once again, moving her eyeballs from side to side to ensure that she was alone, she stepped into the morning room and quickly closed the window behind her.

Thereafter, she tiptoed her way across the room and attached an ear to the door. Hearing nothing, she bravely pulled open the door. This was more difficult considering the bundle she was carrying, but by twisting and turning her fingers awkwardly, she managed to touch the handle with the tip of her thumbs and pushed.

The door swung open easily, and she almost somersaulted into the hallway in surprise.

After calming her jogging heart, she took a deep breath and scurried towards the wooden staircase, turned the corner and finally sprinted towards her room.

It was remarkable. She had managed the entire thing without anyone seeing her, or more importantly, seeing the bundle she was carrying.

She tipped the contents on the floor in her room, a pleased smile on her lips.

She was ready for the next part of the plan.

As she worked, she couldn't help feeling slightly smug. Lady Sedley and Peter had been sitting in the morning room, and they had claimed seeing no one go up the stairs towards Lord Sedley's room at the time he was murdered.

Lucy chuckled. If they admitted that they had not seen anyone go up the stairs, then it was clear who the murderer was. . . or rather, who the murderers were.

Lady Sedley and Peter had killed Lord Sedley.

Lucy added the finishing touches and surveyed herself in the mirror.

Her smile broadened. All she had to do now was to follow Lady Sedley around. The woman was bound to let something slip or try and talk to Peter about it.

And for that, Lucy's attire was perfect. She could shadow Lady Sedley with no fear of being seen. She was as good as invisible.

For Lucy had disguised herself as a tree.

Chapter 15

"Ack." Elizabeth muffled a screech.

"Blargh," Lucy softly exclaimed.

"What in the devil's name have you done to yourself?" Elizabeth growled.

Lucy inched her head out from behind the scantily clad statue of Apollo. "I don't know what you mean."

"Why are you dressed like an unwashed potato?"

"I am not dressed like a potato."

"You look like one."

Lucy shook a branch at Elizabeth. "Potatoes do not have leaves or stems protruding out of them."

"A turnip then."

A twig poked Lucy in the eye. She straightened the branch atop her bonnet that kept dipping and sourly faced Elizabeth. "Why are you lurking in the hallway?"

Elizabeth scowled. "I can do as I please. This is my house." She added as an afterthought, "Miss Turnip."

"But why are you scuttling around on all fours?"

"I dropped an earring, Miss Turnip."

"Shall I help you look for it?" Lucy asked witheringly.

"No, Miss Turnip."

"Are you certain?"

"Go away."

"Truly?"

"Yes."

"Don't be shy."

"I do not," Elizabeth snarled, "want your help."

"I never offered to help you."

"You did."

Lucy stuck her tongue out. "Liar, liar, chicken little vampire."

"What?"

"What, what?"

"Leave," Elizabeth fumed.

"Not leave but leaves, I have leaves stuck all over."

"That is not what I meant, and you know it."

"Do I?"

"Yes, you do."

"I do what?"

"Aaaargh"

Lucy smirked and turned away to look towards the main entrance. Elizabeth had been trying to rile her up by calling her all sorts of vegetables. Hah! Now that same pestering snoot looked ready to explode into several angry pieces.

Her grin widened as the angry, snorting noises continued behind her. She ignored them and instead focused on what was going on downstairs.

Hodgson was standing with the door open. Lady Sedley appeared to be giving him some instructions while he was nodding vigorously in response.

Lucy arched her neck like an inquisitive flamingo. A moment later, just as she had expected, Lady Sedley, wrapped in a scarlet coat with a small black hat perched atop her blonde head, walked out into the sunshine.

Lucy gathered her skirts and stepped out from behind the statue.

Elizabeth, too, stood up, and after throwing Lucy, a final disgusted look pelted down the stairs.

Lucy frowned. Was Elizabeth planning to shadow her mother as well?

There was only one way to find out. She shuffled her way to the top of the stairs.

The next part was more difficult. Her makeshift costume would allow her to blend in with nature easily enough. Once out in the open, she could mingle with the trees and the buds, flit about the garden like a wood nymph and call upon sparrows, squirrels and bees.

But inside Rudhall manor she stood out like a dog with two tails, a bird with teeth or a skinny elephant.

Lucy had been right to be fearful. A person wearing twigs and things did stand out when walking down a grand oak staircase whose fifth, seventh and twelfth step creaked under stress.

And Susan, the upper housemaid who had a remarkable talent of efficiently transforming from a lady's maid into a washerwoman at a moment's notice, was no exception. She swooned at the sight of Lucy drifting down the stairs.

But before the maid had entirely collapsed in a dead faint, she managed to let out a blood-curdling scream that seemed to imply that Aunt Sedley's ghost had sprouted from the ground like a living shrub.

Lucy was annoyed. She would have preferred if the woman had likened her to a majestic tree rather than a shrub.

Another squawk from the maid echoed around the manor.

Lucy frowned harder. She had no time to waste. The full-throated cry the woman had let out before draping herself on the sofa was blasted inconvenient. And the squawk that followed would no doubt bring the other servants whizzing into the room at any moment.

She hitched up her skirts and flew down the stairs uncaring of the fact that the carefully attached leaves had unglued from her skirts, the twigs detached from her bodice, and the tiny white flowers that she had so prettily arranged in her hair tangled together to form an unattractive lump.

Once outdoors, Lucy lurched towards the nearest tree and hid behind it. Parting the branches, she peeked down the lane.

She spotted Lady Sedley's scarlet cloak flash around the corner.

Elizabeth was nowhere in sight.

Breaking off two leafy branches from the tree, she held them in front of her face and scuttled forward from bush to shrub until once again Lady Sedley appeared in front of her.

Lucy sucked in a breath and advanced forward, imagining herself to be a seed-eating plumed guinea hen. She ducked her featherless head and winged her way from thicket to thicket, tree to tree, her eyes watering from the effort of keeping Lady Sedley in view.

No ground-nesting bird weighing a few pounds and found in Sub-Saharan Africa could have spotted a worm with the sort of eyesight Lucy possessed. She cursed her weak vision, annoyed at the disadvantage.

She now decided that she was no longer a plumed guinea hen but a bounding kangaroo. This seemed to work better. She could feel the bounce in her toes and the spring in her step. Pleased, she skipped over stones and hedges trying to guess where Lady Sedley was headed.

Lady Sedley sped down the path taking short, quick steps. She seemed to be making her way towards the old stables, which as far as Lucy knew were overgrown and abandoned.

A few minutes later, Lucy became certain that she was right. Lady Sedley was heading to the stables. Surely only some shady business would take Lady Sedley to this part of the grounds for, after all, the Yellow Garden was far prettier and frequented more often.

Lucy eagerly scuttled forward, her nose sniffing something clandestine in the air, and in her eagerness, she almost missed the fact that Lady Sedley had halted. She stifled a squeal, ducked behind a sizeable prickly bush and peeked out.

Lady Sedley was rapidly shuffling backwards away from the sharp bend in the road. A moment later, she paused and tilted her head as if listening for something.

Lucy dared to move closer. What had caught Lady Sedley's interest? Curious to see what lay beyond the curve in the path, she inched her way towards a tree shaped like a gouty foot that stood a little ahead of Lady Sedley.

With her heart in her tonsils, Lucy squatted, and then gingerly lifting her toes scurried past Lady Sedley. "I am a tree, an invisible tree, a tree . . . a tree, don't see me," she silently chanted.

A leaf crunched, and Lucy's toe froze in mid-air.

Lady Sedley's head jerked up. She furtively looked around for the source of the noise.

Lucy stopped breathing.

By some miracle, Lady Sedley failed to spot Lucy's frightened form trembling a few feet away from her. With a final quick glance at her surroundings, she went back to eavesdropping.

Droplets of sweat were trickling down the side of Lucy's face by the time she managed to creep up to her tree of choice. She brushed them aside and placing her paws on the tree trunk edged her quivering nose forward.

Ian was back.

He was standing with his foot up on a rock, his black hair slicked back and plastered to his head. His scalp glowed white in the sunlight where his oiled hair parted in the middle.

He seemed to be arguing with a fellow blessed with three chins.

The chins jiggled as the man made a threatening gesture.

Ian's shoulders straightened, and he thrust his chest out like an agitated goose. If he had wings, he would have flapped them at this point.

Lucy's nose retreated, and her ear took its place. It was no use. She could hear nothing. She was momentarily distracted when Spinoza suddenly fluttered down from above and settled on her bonnet. The silly raven was no doubt delighted to find branches sticking out of his favourite perch, and he settled in for a long snooze.

Lucy glared at the bird and bobbed her head to dislodge him. She waved her hands on top of her head, twisted her bonnet round and round and finally lifted the bonnet clean off her head.

Spinoza eyed her sourly, his claws digging deep into the bonnet.

Lucy blew into the bird's face.

The raven squawked in protest.

Lady Sedley gave a startled hop and swiveled her head towards the tree-shaped in the form of a gouty foot.

Lucy slowly slithered down the side of the tree trunk.

When Lady Sedley looked back towards Ian, he had already departed with the dumpy man running after him. With another wary glance at the tree, Lady Sedley continued her way to the stables.

Lucy took a deep breath and depositing the bonnet, and the disgruntled raven atop her head once again crept after Lady Sedley.

Outside the stable was an ornate iron bench. And on that bench sat Peter.

Lucy's eyes widened at her good luck as Lady Sedley went and sat down next to her son.

Chapter 16

Lucy snuck behind the stables, walked further down the path and crossed over to the other side. She then backtracked to reach a large fat elm that grew right behind the bench on which Peter and Lady Sedley were sitting.

She plastered her front to the tree trunk and poked her head out from the side to look at the back of their heads.

One of her branches scraped the tree.

Peter glanced back, his eyes narrowed.

She stopped breathing, wondering if he had seen her. It seemed not for he turned back to his mother.

He took a pinch of snuff and delicately held it to his nose with skeletal fingers. "We could have spoken in the house."

"Too many ears," Lady Sedley replied.

"What is it, Mother?"

"Have you taken the jewels?" she asked bluntly.

"I am now the owner of Rudhall and all it contains. Why would I need to steal from myself?"

Lady Sedley replied broodingly, "I cannot understand how it happened? The only person I can trust is you since we were together at the time your father was murdered. I know we did not do it, but I am worried. What if it was one of your siblings?"

Peter closed the snuff box and replaced it in his pocket. He raised his face to the sky. "I was certain this morning it was going to storm this afternoon."

Lady Sedley pulled at the edge of her glove as if it was too tight. "But how could they have gone past without us seeing anything? How do you think they did it?"

Peter shook his head. "And now, look, not a cloud in the sky. I would have had to stay the night in the animal house if it had stormed. The animals become frightened easily and a part of the roof leaks—"

Lady Sedley grabbed his arm and shook it slightly. "You have to help me find the jewels."

He blinked in surprise. "Do you want to find the jewels or the murderer?"

"I want to find the jewels and protect my children if they killed him."

"I see," Peter said, a curious note in his voice.

"You need to forget about your animals and stand by your family instead. Lord Adair has always found the culprit, and if it is Elizabeth or Ian, then we have to find out before he does and help them escape the country."

"This sudden affection, this interest in involving me in your affairs . . . I hope, Mother, it is not because I am now the master of the house."

"Don't be ridiculous, Peter. You are my son—"

Peter leapt up. "I need to see my animals."

"I will make more of an effort—"

"I have asked you six times in the last month to come and see the kittens that I have recently procured. You have ignored me every single time. You have never taken an interest in my affairs, so why should I involve myself in yours?"

"I will come and see them . . . I will make more of effort. We will all come."

"Good day, Mother."

Lady Sedley gripped his sleeve, refusing to let him leave. "Don't be ridiculous. This is about your brother and sister. How can you be so childish—?"

"Good evening."

Lucy started and turned towards the voice. Her eyes widened below her lopsided bonnet, and she inhaled sharply.

Lord Adair stood before them wearing a thick, luxurious dark blue wool coat with large collars and cuffs adorned with glittering silver buttons and dove grey embroidery. A light waistcoat peeked out from behind the coat, beautiful leather gloves covered his long fingers, and his muscled legs were clad in dark buckskin breeches and spotless grey riding boots.

The robes he had worn previously became a distant memory for all those who looked upon him now.

Lucy's eyes glazed over, and she wiped away a touch of drool near the corner of her mouth. He was just so . . . so . . . well proportioned.

"We were just leaving." Lady Sedley discordant voice wriggled its way into Lucy's besotted ears. "I apologise for my curtness, Lord Adair, but it is a bitter day, is it not? I am in a rush to get warm and indoors."

Lord Adair bowed, his eyes lingering on her scarlet coat. "You don't need to apologise. No doubt, the cold is affecting your delicate health."

She flushed. "Yes, well," Her hand stroked the coat, "I was distraught after the funeral. I didn't realise I picked up the red instead of the black—"

Lord Adair shrugged and said blandly, "You don't have to explain. No doubt, grief has sapped you of your ability to perceive the difference between colours."

"The sun is sinking rapidly," she said in confusion. Her limbs jerked awkwardly as she stood up. "I will see you at dinner?"

Lord Adair bowed once more.

Peter, with an incoherent mumbled apology, caught his mother's arm and led her towards the manor.

"Peter is shy in front of all strangers, is he not?"

Lucy glanced around. She could see no one. Who in the world was Lord Adair talking to?

"He is remarkable with animals. Gentle, kind and confident, and yet around humans, he becomes a frightened filly."

Lucy stopped herself from nodding in time. A nodding tree wouldn't have looked right.

"He seems to like you. How long did it take before he opened up to you? And I hear Ian has returned."

The raven woke up and hopped onto her shoulder. Lucy shared a puzzled glance with the bird. Was the cold pushing Lord Adair over the edge? Was she witnessing a man slowly losing his mind in front of her very eyes?

"Peter saw you, Miss Trotter. How could he not spot such an odd-looking tree? The leaves do not match, you have procured different branches from different trees, and your black shoes peeking out under your brown skirts are stark against the snow."

Lucy shuffled out in annoyance. "Lady Sedley did not see me. I think it worked remarkably well."

He smiled and offered her his arm. "I have always wanted to stroll with a wood nymph."

Lucy threw the branch she was holding in her hand and grabbed his arm in relief. Warmth emanated from him in waves, and she sighed in pleasure.

His hard muscles rippled under her fingers and she flushed, becoming warmer still. "The lace near your collar is divine," she gibbered to hide her confusion.

"You have a good eye," he said thoughtfully. "This lace carries an enchanting tale."

"Tell me."

He looked down at her. "Once upon a time, beautiful young women with streams of golden hair were stolen from their English homes and brought over to Greece on a gilded ship. They were then set to work, and the result of their hard labour was a bolt of precious lace. I procured this bit from them for a very high sum."

Her eyes widened. "Truly?"

"No."

She stared out into the distance. "Well, the dress I am wearing was made by a young woman. Not beautiful, but plain and loving . . . a friend." She gulped emotionally. "She was very ill at the time. I would sit by her and sings songs for her while she worked on my dress. It may not look beautiful, but its value is hidden in every single thread. She died soon after making it."

"Truly?" he asked, raising an eyebrow.

"No."

They walked in silence for some time.

"What sort of a tree nymph do I remind you off?" she asked, skirting a wooden log fallen in the path.

ANYA WYLDE

"Erato."

"And you are Arcas?"

He smiled reluctantly.

She caught her breath, "A few married people in my village . . . they looked similar."

"Eh?"

"People, they are young, they get married, and then after a few years, they both start looking the same. The man looks like the woman, and the woman looks like the man, and even the pets in the house start looking like their owners, and before you know it everyone in the family looks like the same person just wearing dresses, breeches or fur."

"I have noticed that."

"Do you think," she asked hopefully, "that if I flutter around you long enough, some of your beauty will spill over to me in a similar manner?"

His smile widened. "You are bewitching, Miss Trotter."

"I don't believe you."

He shrugged.

She frowned. "Aren't you going to convince me otherwise?"

"It would take an entire lifetime to convince a woman of her beauty, and even then she would doubt it."

"I have a gap in my front teeth."

"I know."

"That is not attractive."

"No, it is delightful."

ANYA WYLDE

"Truly?"

"Yes."

"You are not lying?"

"No."

"Are you certain?"

"Yes."

"You don't sound certain."

"Miss Trotter." He pressed his lips together.

She squinted as the sun brightened and bounced off the snow. "That certain was a very uncertain certain. I don't think you were certain. You just said you were certain to make me think that you were certain when, in fact, you were not certain."

"Are you trying to test my patience?" he asked in a soft warning tone.

"You were certain," she assured him hurriedly.

After that, they walked the rest of the way in silence and entered the house together.

Lady Sedley met them near the door. She reeled back at the sight of Lucy, and her mouth fell open in shock. After a tense moment, she used a word Lucy had only heard the servants utter before.

Lucy giggled. Dressed up like a tree with a raven on her head and holding a handsome man's arm . . . She completely agreed with Lady Sedley.

Lawks! It truly was.

Chapter 17

Rudhall Manor was in mourning.

Lady Sedley floated around the house wearing a long black silk dress cut enticingly low. Her chalky complexion contrasted so well with the black that she could have blended in with the walls.

She finally sank into a pale pink armchair placed near the window in the morning room and expertly arranged her head in such a way that the bright sun bathed her skin in the most flattering light. She spent the rest of the day watching the snow melt with an occasional well-timed tear leaking down one green eye.

Elizabeth, on the other hand, did not sink into a single chair the entire day. Instead, she marched purposefully around the house wearing a simple high neck morning dress with a stern collar and lots and lots of buttons.

The servants took one look at her tightly scraped back blonde hair and cowered in the kitchens sending only the bravest to serve her.

Peter Sedley, the spanking new lord of the manor who had recently been slapped with numerous unwanted and futile titles, slinked off to the animal house where he spent the day twitching, flickering and lurching amongst nests and things.

Lastly, Ian percolated for a while on the couch in the library until he nodded off with a half-finished cigar clutched between his maroon fingers.

Meanwhile, Lucy spent the day gently simmering on the bed in her room. She had spent the last few hours peering at the large window above her desk watching the sun lazily drift by, finding shapes in the clouds and counting grey pigeons.

A thin blue quilt was flung across her legs, keeping away the slight nip in the air. A black ribbon tied to her arm kept slipping down to her elbows, and the pillows stacked up behind her back were flattened from lying against them for so long.

On the side table next to her untidy bed sat a fresh apple core, a flickering candle whose melted wax had leaked onto the wood, a cup with dregs of cold tea and a few colourful threads.

After so many hours of idleness, her face had relaxed into a blank, almost spiritual expression. Her mouth hung partially open, her eyes were glazed and unseeing, while her fingers listlessly tweaked a pug's ear.

And it wasn't just her feeling languorous that day. A sort of lethargy had shrouded the entire house ever since the funeral. The walls seem to sulk, the curtains wilt, and as for the furniture . . . why the chair was as depressed as could be and the beds appeared to creak pathetically.

Lucy picked up the apple core and nibbled on it. She had abandoned the idea of disguises, but that did not mean she had abandoned the investigation.

No, she had another plan.

She turned towards the window. The sun had finally dived out of sight, and a far away yellow lamp glowed like an orb in the dark landscape.

She stared at the glistening black glass, wondering what hour it was. The dinner bell rang that very moment jerking her awake. Her eyes unglazed, and her back straightened.

It was time.

"My poor head," Lucy moaned as she lurched into the kitchen.

The cook's face softened slightly.

"I don't think I can join the family for dinner," Lucy continued, her hand stroking her temple. She squinted at the cook, hopefully. "Is there something small for dinner that I can take to my room? I think I am going to retire early tonight."

Rose bared her teeth at the cook in a warning.

Torn, the cook looked from Rose to Lucy. Finally, she pressed her lips together and taking out some bread and cheese placed it next to the meat pie that was meant to be carried into the dining room for the family.

"Is that for me?" Lucy asked in a small voice.

The cook grunted and turned back to poke the fire. Rose, too, ignored Lucy, choosing to pummel the dough instead.

Now that no one was looking at her, Lucy's back straightened, and the pained, pinched look vanished from her eyes. She gleefully picked up the meat pie and pretending not to hear the cook's shout to take the bread instead bounded back to her room.

Once inside, she pulled out a dark blue shawl and laid it on the floor. She put a small cushion, a thin grey quilt and the meat pie on top of the shawl and tied it all together. Throwing the bundle over her shoulder, she slithered out of her room.

The family was busy eating dinner and the servants busy serving them, which was why Lucy was able to stroll across the hallway and into Lady Sedley's rooms without being seen by a single soul.

Lady Sedley's room was impressively large . . . and cold, Lucy added to herself, as a thin worm-like fog escaped her mouth.

She craned her neck. The ceiling was high with a large damp patch in the shape of a broom adorning the centre.

Massaging the muscles in the back of her neck, she eyed the dull rose curtains speculatively. They seemed thick, broad and long enough to conceal a person effectively. She pushed them aside and was disappointed to find no bay window.

She turned back towards the room.

The carpet matched the curtains. They, too, were a dull rose colour patterned with soft green leaves.

She moved closer to the long fragile dressing table placed in the corner. A tallow burning in a long silver candlestick placed in the centre of it illuminated the various thingamabobs lying on the table.

She peered at the glittering pearl comb, sniffed a pot of rouge and frowned at a glass bottle labelled 'Moonlit Drops'.

She reluctantly put the pomatum for unruly hair back on the table and turned her attention towards the large four-poster bed.

She paled. And it wasn't the pastel pillows and lacy cushions sitting uncomfortably atop a somewhat masculine-looking bed that sucked all the air out of her.

No, it was a sharp-faced woman wearing an old fashioned ball gown and a towering powdered wig hovering three and a half feet over the bed that petrified her.

"My dear, Miss Trotter," Aunt Sedley said in ghostly sarcasm, "can it be that you are frightened yet again? I thought we went through this business the last time."

"Glug," Lucy managed.

Aunt Sedley lay down in mid-air and rested her chin on her palms. "Oh, smooth your hair. I don't like seeing it wave at the roof. It makes you look eerie."

Lucy grabbed her terrified hair and forced it back into a bun.

"Better," Aunt Sedley commented. "Now, how far have you progressed in your investigations?"

"Glug."

Aunt Sedley snapped her fingers. "I don't have the luxury to hover until you get over your unreasonable fear, girl. Now, form coherent sentences and tell me your plan."

"I followed Lady Sedley this afternoon," Lucy wheezed out. She was still reeling from the ghostly vision, and the sound of her own voice surprised her so much that she was spooked into silence once again.

"You followed her and . . . what did you see?" Aunt Sedley asked in a gentler, more encouraging tone.

A deep, steadying breath later, Lucy blurted out, "She met Peter near the old stables, and from the conversation, I gathered that she and Peter were innocent. She thinks it could be one of her other children who have killed Lord Sedley."

Aunt Sedley rolled on her back and produced a ghostly cigar. "Then what, pray tell, my lovely child, are you doing in Lady Sedley's room. Didn't you cross her off your suspects' list?"

Lucy shook her head. "What if she knew that I had been following her? Lord Adair said that Peter saw me. What if they staged the entire conversation for my benefit?"

Aunt Sedley blew rings of green smoke. "Aren't you a clever thing?"

Feeling braver, Lucy said, "My plan is simple. I am going to hide under the bed and wait for Lady Sedley to spill all her secrets in the arms of the valet."

Aunt Sedley nodded appreciatively. "If not a confession, then Margaret may let slip a few clues under the valet's adventurous fingertips."

Lucy blushed.

Aunt Sedley rolled back over and waved the cigar in her direction. "Move, Miss Trotter. Go on . . . get under the bed. Stop mooning about."

Lucy opened her bundle and unpacked the things. She wriggled under the bed and lay down on the blue shawl. The quilt kept her warm, while the cushion went under her head.

Aunt Sedley's head detached itself from its body and appeared next to Lucy.

Lucy reeled back startled by the disembodied head hovering next to her.

Aunt Sedley didn't seem to notice her discomfort. She calmly inspected Lucy's handiwork and nodded her ghostly head in satisfaction.

"The bed has plenty of room underneath," Aunt Sedley said. "It is a tad dusty, though. Eat your meat pie. I will float around and keep you company. I always hated eating alone when I was alive. It made me feel most depressed.

Lucy obediently bit into the pie. It was delicious.

"You have a crumb on your chin," Aunt Sedley pointed out.

Lucy wiped it off. "How is it that you don't know who killed your brother? Didn't you ask him?

"He said he was asleep when he was attacked. By the time he came awake, he had already been stabbed, and his assailant had disappeared. Then he died."

"Well, didn't you see the murderer?"

"I am not omnipresent, idiot. I was asleep at the time."

Lucy chewed thoughtfully. "Do all spirits sleep during the day?"

"No, we prefer sunlight. As you can tell," Aunt Sedley said, producing her disembodied arm and waving it in front of Lucy's horrified face, "we are almost transparent, and the sunlight makes us completely invisible. Also, the heat of the sun negates the coldness humans feel in our presence, which is why most ghosts prefer roaming around in the daylight."

"So I could be sharing a bench with a ghost during the day, and I wouldn't know it?"

"Precisely . . . or many ghosts. Some of them do like to huddle together."

"But then why were you asleep when the murder occurred? It happened during the day."

"Because ghosts that want to scare people sleep during the day and wake during the night. I had to change my hours because of Margaret. I was keeping an eye on her every night, trying to frighten her away from the valet . . . for Roo Roo's sake."

"Thank you for explaining."

Aunt Sedley's hand detached itself from her body and flew over to affectionately pat Lucy on the head.

Lucy's facial muscles froze in fright. She didn't dare twitch during the entire patting process.

Aunt Sedley screwed her head and arm back onto her hovering body and floated up and towards the door, "Now, I am going to go and listen in on the conversation in the dining room. I will be back . . . back . . . back."

Aunt Sedley faded away, and with her departure, heat whizzed back into the room. But it wasn't enough. Lucy's fingers remained icy and fearful. She rubbed her palms together and blew on it.

Her heart was still racing.

Aunt Sedley was a ghost.

She truly existed.

It had not been a dream.

Belatedly, Lucy pulled the quilt up and over her head in fright.

Do not think about it, she firmly told herself. Stop trembling, she ordered her hands. Perhaps she had fallen asleep while waiting for Lady Sedley, she consoled her terrified mind. It had all been a dream.

She pinched herself and yelped. She was awake. She was not asleep and had not been sleeping.

A ghost had indeed spoken to her.

She popped her head out from under the quilt, but her eyes remained squeezed shut. She would panic later after this entire ordeal was over. After the murderer was found.

For the moment, she must focus on the task at hand. All she had to do was stay quiet, be patient and listen hard.

An hour later, she was still quiet, being patient and listening hard, and with every passing moment, fear seeped out of her skin replaced by calmness and finally boredom.

Every sound was amplified in the silence. The howl of a dog outside, a wife chasing a husband around in the village, and footsteps padding along in the corridors...

Footsteps in the corridor? Lucy's ears twitched in anticipation.

Sure enough, feminine feet entered the room.

Lucy deflated.

The feet were clad in sensible black shoes, the bottom of the skirts was dull and grey, but most importantly, the creature was whistling.

Ladies did not whistle.

It was a blasted maid who had come in to light a fire.

The maid soon departed, and boredom skipped back into the room.

The fire roared, and Lucy watched the dancing flames until her eyes began to droop.

Chapter 18

The sun was running around in circles in the sky, and Lucy was deliciously baking in the hot sand. The cool water of the sea occasionally came over to give her toes a playful lick, while twelve fairies fluttered about her holding golden plates laden with fruits, ices and cold meats.

It was a beautiful little spot far away from noise and chaos. A tiny little paradise that was wrenched away from time and hurled atop a happy little cloud that lazily drifted along the cornflower blue sky.

The sun smiled widely increasing the temperature by a few more comfortable degrees. She rolled over drowsily, the sand particles surrounding her rolled over as well. The clean, dry sand was now facing upwards and sparkling like new.

It was a self-refreshing bed, an ingenious product created by dreamland.

She smiled contently and reached for one of the colourful drinks knocking against each other above her head.

The crystal glasses clinked and clanked together, making beautiful music while the vibrant coloured liquids in the glass bubbled and twinkled in the golden light.

Her hand curled around a sapphire hued drink, but before she could taste it, a horrifying screech pierced the air.

The fairies flew away, the clouds rushed to cover the sun, and the happy little cloud disintegrated.

She woke with a soft annoyed snort and rubbed her crusty eyes.

There was barely any light wherever she was . . . and she was lying on something hard.

She blinked away the sleep, wondering if she had nodded off in Miss Summer's downstairs cupboard with yet another stolen rice pudding.

It was another few moments before she came fully awake and recalled where she was. Under Lady Sedley's bed.

And she was no longer alone. Someone else was in the room with her.

Her heart started beating loudly as the familiar sounds of someone getting ready for bed reached her ears.

Small delicate feet clad in white satin slippers neared the bed.

That, Lucy thought, had to be Lady Sedley.

"Get the robe, or I will fling you out of the window," screeched a girlish voice.

That, Lucy nodded, was definitely Lady Sedley.

The ghost of Aunt Sedley manifested itself next to Lucy's head and put a translucent finger to her lips in warning.

Lucy gulped. She was beginning to feel like a tightly corked bottle of champagne that had just been shaken.

She willed herself to breathe slowly and softly.

Lucy willed and willed and willed. She tried to let not one breath escape that was too loud, too wheezy or too gaspy. But as it often happens, trying to breathe softly or not breathe at all makes one want to open their mouth and gulp in air as if they were drowning.

Lucy was drowning, and before she knew it, she was also panting.

And she was not the only one who was panting. She had been so focused on the satin clad feet that she had failed to notice the two pugs that had sneaked into the room behind Lady Sedley.

The pugs now moved their heads from side to side, no doubt wondering why in the world a human being was lying under the bed and not on top of it.

They spotted Aunt Sedley's disembodied head floating next to Lucy's right ear, and their short little tails immediately drooped, their fur stood up straight, and their tongues retreated back into their mouths. The pugs now looked like confused miniature lions.

"Maggie, darling." The valet entered the room.

"I have been waiting," Lady Sedley breathed huskily.

ANYA WYLDE

The sounds of kissing and sighs reached Lucy's ears, and she wished she could see what was going on.

"The funeral is over," Lady Sedley was saying. "It is a pity I have to wear black for the next year."

"I adore you in black," the valet whispered.

Lucy nervously bit her lip. The pugs' tails had lifted straight up, and their squashed noses were quivering.

"Oh, don't," the valet squealed.

"What is it, Pookey?" Lady Sedley crooned.

"I have a thing here," the valet muttered.

"A thing?"

"You know what I mean," he replied sulkily.

"Oh, you mean the wart on your buttock?" Lady Sedley breathed lustily.

Lucy soundlessly slapped her head. This she did not want to hear.

Aunt Sedley shoved a finger in each year and whizzed out of the room, her ghostly cheeks glowing in the candlelight.

The pugs brightened up.

"Yes," the valet snapped.

"But you went to see the physician. You said it would be fine today," Lady Sedley whined.

"Yes, well, things didn't go well. He rubbed some odd-smelling lotion and now . . . "

"Let me see," she begged.

"No," the valet growled.

"Let me," Lady Sedley giggled.

Lucy watched in horrified silence as two pairs of legs raced around the room. Soon the couple were bouncing on the bed as Lady Sedley tried to pull the valet's pants down to inspect his buttocks.

Meanwhile, the pugs appeared to be storing up a volcano of excitement as they looked from Lady Sedley and the valet fighting with a pair of breeches to Lucy peeking out from between shocked fingers.

"Finally," Lady Sedley crooned.

A brief silence followed this gesticulation.

"Well," the valet broke the silence.

"Yes, it is a funny thing," Lady Sedley said. "It has grown, and now it is almost like a wrinkled red doorknob. Something I would like to grab and pull—"

"No," the valet said hurriedly pulling on his breeches. "I think I will retire for the night.

As you can see I am indisposed—"

"You do not approve of my new white silk chemise then?" Lady Sedley asked throatily.

Lucy twitched as a black silk robe pooled near her worried nose.

At the same time, the pugs seemed to have realised that Lucy was surrounded by crumbs of meat pie. They started sniffing in delight.

The valet sucked in a breath of appreciation.

The pugs bent their front legs and raised up their behinds.

The valet stepped closer to Lady Sedley. "Perhaps if we are careful."

The volcano erupted, and two identical puppies pounced on Lucy in unrestrained rapture.

Lucy froze in horror while the pups tried to shove wet tongues into her ears.

"My love," the valet gasped.

Yap, yap, yap barked the pugs in a paroxysmal of delight.

Lucy softly moaned in despair and closed her eyes.

When she opened them again, she found the valet and Lady Sedley's face floating in front of her face.

"Out," they both snapped in unison.

Lucy crawled out on trembling legs.

"What were you doing?" Lady Sedley asked through clenched teeth.

"Looking for the pugs," Lucy blurted out.

"You must have been under the bed for some time, so why did you not alert me to your presence?"

Lucy looked away from the white silk chemise, which was now forever burned into her mind. She did not know what to say.

Lady Sedley snatched the robe off the ground and slipped it on. She asked the valet to fetch Lord Adair and the rest of the family.

"I saw you romancing the valet," Lucy boldly threatened. "I will tell everyone about it."

"They are not going to believe you, young lady, not anymore."

Chapter 19

"This wicked girl was hiding under the bed, Lord Adair. Do you need any more proof that she is up to no good?" Lady Sedley asked, pawing at his beautifully cut blue velvet evening coat.

Aunt Sedley's spectre glided into the room and positioned itself behind Lord Adair. Her ghostly eyes twinkled at the sight of Lord Adair's firm behind, and she bobbed a little bit in admiration.

Lord Adair took out a cigar and lit it.

Lady Sedley bristled and pawed at the gilt button more insistently. "We are not safe with her in this house. We need to keep her away from the family."

He flicked an impersonal glance towards Lucy. "She cannot leave until I complete my investigations."

Elizabeth reared her head from a chair near Lady Sedley's bed. "But surely you can't mean that? Are we to keep a murderer and a thief lose in our home? What if she was prowling tonight with the intent of choosing her next victim?"

Lady Sedley squeaked and immediately wrapped herself around Lord Adair's arm in fright where she hung bubbling and spluttering like a dozen eggs frying in a hot pan.

Lord Adair ignored the parasite curled around his arm and using his left hand, calmly extracted the cigar from between the fingers of his besmirched right hand. He took a small puff. "Miss Trotter, Miss Sedley is correct. This does not reflect well on your character."

Peter's long grey wool nightcap nodded in agreement.

Lucy's eyes flared in anger. Lord Adair knew she was trying to find the killer. How else was she supposed to discover anything if not by snooping? She hung her head, pretending to be ashamed while calling Lord Adair an infernal scoundrel in her head.

"I say, what are we discussing?" Ian asked. He understood things late or not at all, and when he did understand anything, it was only half of it.

Aunt Sedley bobbed over and stuck her spirit fingers into Ian's ears and pretended to clean them out.

A laugh escaped Lucy's lips frightening all humans present in the room except Lord Adair.

Elizabeth growled impatiently. "Can't you see she is a dangerous loon?" If we cannot throw her out of the house, then I suggest we move her to a room farther away from the family. Perhaps in a different wing?

"We don't have any rooms available," Lady Sedley objected.

"Who is coming to stay?" Ian drawled. Aunt Sedley pushed a phantom handkerchief through one of his ears and pulled it out of the other.

"She can move to the basement, Lord Adair. She can stay with the servants," Elizabeth offered after a brief moment.

Lucy turned a shocked face towards Elizabeth.

Lady Sedley brightened. "That is a splendid suggestion. I can ask my maid to keep an eye on her from now on."

Aunt Sedley produced a ghostly hammer and started walloping Lady Sedley on the head. It didn't hurt Lady Sedley, but the action seemed to give the spirit some sort of morbid satisfaction.

"Allow me to keep an eye on her. She won't hurt the family," Lord Adair smoothly interjected.

Elizabeth's lips tightened, but no one dared to oppose Lord Adair's suggestion.

"But I agree with Miss Sedley," Lord Adair continued, tapping the cigar so that a shower of grey ash melted into the carpet. "Miss Trotter will have to move to the basement before eleven tomorrow morning."

"Ah," Ian came awake, "Miss Trotter is moving to a servant's room. Whatever for?"

"She was caught hiding under mother's bed," Elizabeth snapped at Ian.

Lucy's shoulder sagged, though a part of her admitted that things could have been worse. She could have been locked in a room until Lord Adair finished his investigations.

When she next dared to look up, it was to catch Lady Sedley goggling at Peter trying to communicate something telepathically. Clearly, Ian had inherited his brains from his mother.

"After all the excitement, we need a drop of the strong stuff," Lord Adair remarked. He pulled out a dark bottle from one pocket and a glass from the other. Pouring a generous amount for himself, he handed the bottle to Lady Sedley. "Take a big swig," he encouraged with a kindly look in his eye.

Lady Sedley detached herself from his arm and drank. Colour rushed back into her face, and with eyes crossed, she passed the bottle to Peter.

Once everyone had taken a relaxing gulp, and the bottle had been extracted from Ian's vice-like grip, Elizabeth stood up and smoothed her skirts. "Well, now that is settled," she said, "we can all depart for bed." She caught her brother's arm, while her lashes fluttered helplessly at Lord Adair. "Ian, the hallway is eerily dark. Will . . . will you escort me to my room?"

Lord Adair contemplated the golden liquid in his glass, while Ian looked comically taken aback by the request.

"You are jesting, Lizzy? You are afraid of a dark hallway? Why, you would frighten the ghosts away with that cackling laughter of yours," Ian grinned.

ANYA WYLDE

Aunt Sedley nodded in agreement.

"Allow me," Lord Adair cut in smoothly.

Elizabeth smiled triumphantly as she hooked her claws in Lord Adair's arm. Aunt Sedley smoothed her hair, adjusted her corset and floated out behind them. It seemed even the dead were not immune to Lord Adair's charms.

Ian followed, looking confounded as usual.

Lucy crept out next, and as soon as she had walked a few steps away from the room, a heavy burden seemed to escape the knotted bun at the nape of her neck. She strode swiftly down the hallway only to halt suddenly beside the hideous statue of Medusa.

A vision of Lady Sedley goggling at Peter's woolly nightcap arose in front of her eyes.

She blinked away the image and spun on her heels.

This time her swift walk down the corridor was not towards her room but back from where she had come.

Lucy Anne Trotter had decided to eavesdrop some more.

**

"Ask Lord Adair to cease investigating at once." Lucy overheard Lady Sedley tell Peter.

"Me?" Peter squeaked.

"Yes, you," Lady Sedley snapped. "You are now the owner of Rudhall and all it contains. Stand tall, lift up your weak chin and order that man to leave your property."

"Glurg," Peter managed to say.

"That," Lady Sedley said coldly, "is not helpful."

The silence seemed to stretch.

Peter must be digging deep within his soul, Lucy mused.

Then she heard him ask ever so softly, "But he may find father's killer and the jewels."

"We can find the jewels ourselves. Don't you understand, you fool —"

A rough hand clasped around Lucy's mouth while another caught her around the waist. The stench of smoke and wet dog tickled her nose.

Her eyes grew large in horror as she felt herself being lifted off the ground.

"You are unbelievable," Ian whispered in her ear as he walked down the hallway. "You were banished to the basement for hiding under mother's bed, and here I find you going right back to doing exactly what you were punished for."

Lucy cursed her foolishness. Why, oh why had she been convinced that so soon after her banishment to the servant's room no one would expect her to repeat her offence? She had thought she was being clever.

Ian chuckled and playfully slapped her bottom.

She panicked and began wriggling in his grip like an agitated earthworm and kicked about like an offended vegetarian giraffe.

ANYA WYLDE

Her squirming and flailing did not help. Ian easily carried her down the hallway, turned the corner and flung open the first door on the right.

He threw her inside.

She fell face down.

She heard the bolt shut and realised that Ian had locked the door from the outside. He had left her alone in this strange room which had not a glimmer of light anywhere.

She had just opened her mouth to scream when he returned carrying a candle.

The yellow light cast looming shadows on the wall. It was a room she had never been in before. It was empty of furniture save a cupboard in the corner and a broken table by the window.

His teeth gleamed white as he leered at her.

"He is just like his father." Aunt Sedley floated in through the blank wall. She tilted her head. "Not as dashing though. Do you want to kiss him?"

Lucy shook her head, frantically. "I want to get away."

Ian frowned and took a step towards her. "Don't make a noise or I will tell mother what I saw. And this time your punishment won't be so kind."

"Don't show fear," Aunt Sedley commented sipping from a teacup.

Lucy crossed her arms and looked Ian in the eye. "What do you want?"

"A kiss and cuddle," he replied.

The windows rattled. "That is the best I can do. No pillows, drapes or quilt in this room to frighten him with," Aunt Sedley said stirring sugar in her cup. "The cold is not helping. He is full of lust. He won't feel the chill."

Lucy threw a pleading look in the ghost's direction and took a step back.

Ian took a step forward.

Aunt Sedley sighed. "You should learn how to defend yourself from unwanted advances. I learned it all when I was fifteen. I could have taught you the Hunga Munga, but the tool needed is not at hand, and it will take some time to teach you . . . I could try to explain certain points in the body to attack that will kill him in an instant. I learned that trick from a wonderful lover—"

Ian grabbed Lucy's arm. "Can't you think of something quick?" Lucy squeaked at the ghost.

"Oh, no, my love. This will take some time," Ian breathed into her ear.

Aunt Sedley pursed her lips thoughtfully. "Ah, I think I have it."

"Hurry," Lucy urged.

"Ooh, naughty, naughty," Ian chuckled and licked her earlobe.

Aunt Sedley fluttered down next to Lucy and eyed Ian's busy tongue meditatively, "This is what I think you should do. Bite his arm painfully enough to make him screech and release you. He will be busy letting out a stream of profanities while you race over to the candle lying on the table, pick it up and fling it in his direction. He will squeal in fright and dodge the candle to save his limbs from burning. The candle will fall to the ground and start rolling on the dry wooden floor. He will recall at that crucial moment that when dry wood and a burning candle meet, it usually means a flaming disaster. Predictably, he will scrabble after the candle to save the house from burning down. Meanwhile, you wrench open the door and flee down the hallway. Thereafter, run very fast, for it won't be long before he comes hurtling after you."

"Thank you," Lucy told the spirit.

"You are welcome," Ian replied and chewed her ear lobe more enthusiastically.

After that, it was a simple matter of following Aunt Sedley's directions, which Lucy did beautifully. She bit Ian, flung the candle in his direction and wrenched open the door. And just as Aunt Sedley had predicted, she was soon running down the hallway thanking her stars that Ian was a dimwit.

Dimwit turned out to be quicker than she had expected for his bruised manly ego spurred him on.

He came flying down the corridor like an enraged Viking who had been pinked by a chit of a girl.

His Stone Age ancestors awoke inside his wily soul and reared their angry heads. They bared their sharp teeth and did a fiery little dance.

Encouraged, Ian quickened his pace and ran like he had never run before. The wind rushed through his black hair, making the oily locks streak back and sway to and fro.

Soon his ancestors started singing battle songs inside his empty head. He smiled a grim smile as he bounded forward with his legs spread far and wide.

At this point, his ancestors from the Iron Age joined him as well. They pulled out trumpets, flutes and drums and started playing a perky little tune.

He was now running so fast that his feet were barely touching the ground, his bottom was swinging madly, while his fleshy cheeks were jiggling alarmingly.

Lucy gulped and forced her limbs to accelerate.

He was bigger and faster.

She had to reach her room before he caught her again. A quick glance behind showed he was closing in on her when suddenly a low moan reached her ears. A loud crash followed, and she turned back in time to see Ian lying flat on the ground with Palmer, the baboon, sitting on his back.

Palmer seemed to be picking nits out of Ian's hair and calmly eating them while Ian struggled to get the heavy animal off his back.

She didn't wait to see more but hurtled back to her room.

"Change of plans," she whispered as she threw herself on the bed in relief. "I am going to start searching for the jewels. No more eavesdropping."

"I concur," Aunt Sedley said, swinging upside down from the ceiling.

Chapter 20

"And you can help me look for the jewels," Lucy said, sitting up on the bed and staring up at the spirit slowly revolving near the roof. "You can go anywhere and listen to anyone without being seen. This is perfect."

Aunt Sedley stopped revolving, hooked two of her fingers together and swung from side to side.

"Whose room will you search first?" Lucy prompted.

Aunt Sedley ducked her head, bit her lip and placed her palms on her cheek.

Lucy frowned. "Why are you acting so odd? Are you coming down with some sort of ghostly fever?"

"I am blushing, you nitwit," Aunt Sedley snapped.

"Whatever for?"

"I am sorry. I can't help you search the house."

"You were blushing because you can't help me look for the jewels?"

Aunt Sedley floated down and sat next to Lucy. She giggled. "Well, no . . . I was blushing because—"

"Yes?"

"You would be surprised to know that when I was alive, I was extremely arrogant. I had all sorts of men wanting to marry me, and I refused them all. I believed anyone who was not blue-blooded was not worthy of my affections."

Lucy drummed her fingers on the pillow. "And now that you have no blood—"

"Are you trying to hurt my feelings?"

"I am sorry," Lucy hastily soothed. "I didn't think. Continue."

"After I died," Aunt Sedley resumed reluctantly, "I met someone."

"Someone."

"Mr Brown. He used to be a blacksmith."

"I see."

"Well, we are courting."

"I don't see."

"He is wooing me. I have been spending my evenings with him. It is still so new that I cannot bear to put a stop to our meetings so soon. He has taught me so much . . . for instance how to respect everyone, even commoners. Why do you suppose I don't look down my fine aristocratic nose at you?"

"I see. So, you are being wooed by a Mr Brown, and you would rather haunt the village with him than help me hunt for the jewels. You talk to me like I am a human being and not horse droppings stuck to your translucent boot because of this same Mr Brown?"

"We don't haunt anyone. Just float around clouds and—" She stopped abruptly. "Why are you looking at me so oddly?"

"I didn't know ghosts courted—"

"You don't think we have a heart?"

"Well you are dead so how can you have a—"

"We have emotions."

"I am sorry."

"Do you have to constantly remind me that I am dead?"

"I didn't mean to—"

"Thoughtless. All young women your age are heartless, cold, calculating—"

"No, no, I promise I will be more sensitive. Truly."

"Humph."

"Tell me about Mr Brown. He sounds kind and wonderful and charming. Is he handsome?" Lucy coaxed.

"Mr Brown . . . "Aunt Sedley sighed and sparked a few times before melting into a puddle at the bottom of the bed.

"Aunt Sedley?" Lucy worriedly peered at the sappy pool on the ground.

Like a phoenix rising from the ashes, Aunt Sedley reformed herself after a moment. Her ghostly bosom heaved up and down as she gushed, "Oh, he is handsome, sooo handsome, but what truly attracted me was his cowlick. A wonderful tuft of hair that grows right at the back of his head. It sticks up and trembles every time I go near him."

"Are you meeting him tonight?"

Aunt Sedley squealed and flew towards the window. "I will be late. We were meant to skim over the river tonight. I promised to meet him after dinner. I will be back . . . back . . . back ...."

"Ghosts have dinner?" Lucy muttered to herself. "What in the world do they eat?"

"I heard that." Aunt Sedley's voice floated back.

"I am sorry," Lucy shouted back. This time the rain dancing on the windowpane was her only answer.

***

It was mid-day, and yet the room in the basement was dark enough to warrant a candle. The tiny bed with a hard mattress had a lumpy pillow on one end and a thin blanket folded at the other. A mere two steps away stood a creaking cupboard, an empty basin, and a single chair with chipped flowers and bulbs carved into its back. The room had no windows, and it stank of mould and gin.

Lucy slapped the chair with a rag and dust billowed into her face making her sneeze.

"I see you are settling into your new room."

Lucy whipped around to find Lord Adair standing near the door. She said nervously, "Come in."

His long black cloak rustled as he bent his head to avoid hitting the top of the doorway and entered the room. He straightened up and swept a critical gaze at the contents of the room. "I can arrange for you to move into the attic with the maids instead of ...." He gestured at the blank, windowless wall.

"The maids share a room. I would rather have my privacy," Lucy said, struggling to open the brown travelling bag sitting on the bed.

"I thought as much." He rummaged around in his cloak and pulled out a bundle. "This is for you."

Lucy abandoned the bag, wiped her hands on the side of her skirt and took the offered bundle.

It contained twenty candles tied together with a bit of twine.

Her eyes grew large. "Goodness. These are beeswax."

"And here."He offered her the thick quilt he had been holding in his other hand behind his back. At her questioning look, he clarified. "The cook and the kitchen maid have made their rooms comfortable down here, whereas you are in a peculiar position, and I suspect without any money."

"Thank you," Lucy said, gingerly holding the candles. She had only burned tallow before. "But why did you—?"

"I feel responsible since I agreed with Miss Sedley that you should live in the basement."

"I don't understand you, my lord. One moment you punish me and the next you offer me a salve for my wounds."

"Are you angry," he asked, taking another step towards her. The room seemed to shrink.

She looked away from his penetrating gaze. "No, I am not angry. I am just glad to still have my freedom."

His dark eyes shimmered in the dim light. "Can I ask you a question?"

Lucy nodded and pulled out the rag and attacked the cupboard.

"How can you smile, Miss Trotter?"

Tears suddenly rose up and choked her throat. Her hand faltered in the act of dusting.

She cast around for a change of topic.

A sharp intake of breath later, she spoke in a voice that only slightly wobbled. "Mr Sedley . . . I mean, the younger Mr Sedley is an empty-headed fool."

He smiled. "Trying to change the topic, annoy the other person or baffle them until they forget their original question. It's a special little trick of yours, is it not, Miss Trotter?"

Her eyes widened.

He said kindly, "You don't have to answer my question."

"But will you answer mine?" she asked.

He frowned and gestured for her to continue.

She straightened her back. "Ian is a dimwit."

"No doubt—"

"Then how could he have helped you, my lord, with anything? You said he did you a great service once."

"It is a long story."

Lucy flung the rag into the cupboard and sat down on the bed. "I have time."

A tiny smile teased the corner of his mouth. "Very well, then. Three years ago, on a cold wintry day, I was unclad and hiding in a bush when Mr Sedley's carriage happened to pass by. I waved the carriage down, and Mr Sedley stopped and offered me a cloak and a ride back to my house. He saved me from freezing to death."

"Why were you naked in a bush?" Lucy asked, fascinated.

"I had a friend whose services were no longer needed, and she got wind of the fact before I had confessed it."

"You mean a mistress," Lucy corrected.

He continued on as if she had not spoken. "Next thing I knew my clothes were stolen, my carriage sent away, and I was shivering without a stitch outside my friend's home. I made my way over to the road, and thankfully, Mr Sedley's carriage happened to come along. He understood my plight, considering he had been at the receiving end of a similar plot."

"You were lucky," Lucy mused. "A man with wit would have never halted a carriage for an unclothed man running around bushes."

He inclined his head. "True. Which is why I am indebted to Mr Sedley and would like to repay him. He did all he could to help me."

"I don't like Mr Sedley," Lucy said, recalling the previous night's incident.

A faint frown creased his forehead.

She turned back towards the cupboard and picked up the rag. "Thank you once again for the candles and the quilt, my lord."

A soft sigh escaped him. "Miss Trotter, things would be much simpler if you have a little faith in my honesty and ability. I will not let you hang if you are innocent."

Lucy squeezed her eyes shut. His dark voice lured her into believing him. Also, it was steadily becoming more and more difficult sharing such a small space with him. He seemed to be engulfing her from all sides . . . She gripped her skirts, threw back her head and belted out a song.

Yoodle yoodle yoo,
Deedle deedle den.
I am a happy angel,
Who fell from sweet heaven,
My belly full of beer,
Too heavy for wispy clouds to bear,
My fingers too chubby to pluck the delicate harp,
I fell, and I fell, and I fell.
Yoodle yoodle yoo,
Deedle deedle den.
I am the happy angel—

Lord Adair took a step back. "Miss Trotter, what the devil are you doing?"

Lucy paused. "I am singing, my lord."

"But why?"

"I have been told I have a lovely voice. I can sit nearby when you eat your dinner every evening and sing like an angel. It will soothe your tortured soul."

"My soul is not tortured," he said, taking another cautious step back.

"I can play the harpsichord, speak a little bit of French, dance and sing. According to Miss Summer, I make a pleasant and humorous companion. I can pop out now and then to entertain you all for the price of twenty pounds a year. I confess I am offering my services rather cheap but considering the circumstances . . . My lord?"

Lord Adair had disappeared.

All at once, the room seemed to grow bigger and lighter.

Lucy hugged herself, pleased that she still had the power to baffle, frighten or confound people and that Lord Adair was no exception. Considerably cheered, she turned towards the bed.

Her eyes widened in shock.

The travel bag which she had been struggling with for the last hour lay open. How in the blooming daisies she wondered in amazement had Lord Adair managed it without her seeing him move so much as an inch towards the bed?

***

ANYA WYLDE

The servant's room was not bad, Lucy mused, chewing the back of a pencil. True, she had no window, but the bed was a good size, and in the corner, she even had a chair.

She pulled out what was left of the pencil with a loud pop and began scribbling on the sheet of paper. Anyone could have stolen the jewels. The thief had a whole day and night to do it. The question was, how?

She absently scratched over Peter and Lady Sedley's name with the pencil until the names were blackened out. The theft had to have occurred after the murder since Lord Sedley had worn the key even while bathing.

So, she pursed her lips thoughtfully, he had been murdered, the key was taken off from around his neck, the jewels stolen and the key replaced—all within one hour and without anyone seeing the culprit.

Therefore, it stood to reason that the person who killed Lord Sedley currently had the jewels in his or her possession. All she had to do was find the jewels, and she would find the murderer.

It was a pity she hadn't been able to search Lord Sedley's room for clues after his death. The valet and the butler had taken turns, making sure no one entered the room.

A sharp rap on the door made her jump.

Peter stood near the partially open door.

She shoved the list under the pillow and stood up. "Come in, my lord." A hint of irritation laced her voice. She wondered why everyone now assumed that they could come calling to her bedroom whenever they pleased.

"I am sorry," Peter mumbled at once. "I shouldn't have come."

She waited for him to leave. He didn't.

After a minute of turning his hat round and round in his hand, he said, "I wanted to ask if you needed help."

Her eyebrow rose. "I am fine. Thank you for your concern, my lord."

His forehead creased. "My lord . . . it sounds odd. I am still not used to being Lord Sedley . . . I wish . . . " He trailed off.

"Is there anything else?"

"No." He turned to go but seemed to change his mind. He jerked back around and asked in a feverish voice, "Did you take the jewels?"

"I did not," she replied slowly.

"I see." He did not look like he believed her. The hat slipped from his hand, and he bent to pick it up. A slight flush stained his cheeks. His fingertips touched the brim, and he spoke without looking up. "If you ever need help, Miss Trotter, I am here for you."

Lucy blushed in response. She noted once again how attractive he was.

He looked up and caught her eye. "If you need to run . . . I can help."

The blush melted into confusion. She shook her head.

He waited for her to speak, and when she didn't, he bowed and departed.

Lucy walked over to the door and closed it. She pressed her forehead against the dark wood in confusion.

Why did Peter want to help her? Why would he want his father's murderer to escape?

And if he did want to help her, then all he had to do was to send Lord Adair away and stop the investigations . . . or could he?

Was Peter Sedley in love with her? Is that why—?

She quickly stamped out the last thought. She needed to focus on one thing at a time, and currently, she aimed to search all the servants' rooms.

Peter Sedley was a tangle that could be unravelled at a more appropriate time.

Chapter 21

Lucy paused mid crawl. She was on her way up to the attic to rummage through the maid's belongings, but the sight of Lord Adair in his room arrested her.

She moved closer to the slight opening in the door and inched her nose inside.

Lord Adair was resplendent in his dark evening attire. His eyes were closed, hands folded, and he was standing on his left leg while the other hovered in mid-air. And as she watched, he slowly switched legs, and now stood on his right leg.

She shook her head. The man was supposed to be investigating. He was meant to catch the murderer and save her neck from the noose. Instead, he was doing the most demented things, and come to think of it, she had never seen him prowl, nose or sweat for clues.

"Hurry before the maids return from dinner," he drawled without opening his eyes.

She stifled a gasp and stared hard at his eyelashes. They were thick, casting feathery shadows on his cheeks and definitely resting against his skin. Could the man see with closed eyes?

"Stop goggling," he urged, his eyeballs shifting urgently behind tightly shut lids.

Lucy's nose quickly retreated from the room and taking his advice, she sprinted up the stairs.

Half an hour later, she stood glaring at the room in the attic. She had poked and prodded the bricks in the wall, peeked under the mattress, explored the insides of the chimney, tried to lift the wooden floorboards, looked for an opening at the back of the cupboard, checked under the dust-laden rug and even inspected the bottom of the basin.

She had found a few coppers, a pair of Lady Sedley's lost satin slippers, Elizabeth's missing rouge pot, a broken comb, old ribbons, and for some odd reason Ian's favourite breeches and shoes.

She huffed in annoyance. Her long brown hair had long escaped its pins, her face and hands were coated with soot, and in spite of it being midwinter, she was sweating.

Jabbing a tongue between the gap in her teeth, she paused to think.

Jenny, who had usually dusted and swept Lord Sedley's room and had deftly avoided his lusty kisses, was Lucy's main suspect. The buxom young girl could have taken the key out while consenting to a kiss. She had sharp eyes, quick fingers and was said to be ambitious.

Or it could be Susie who shared the room with Jenny. Though not as pretty and a good deal more bitter, she too had reason to visit Lord Sedley's room. She did the laundry and made up the beds.

Lucy squinted at the two neat little beds, the small cupboard, and the two polished chairs by the low window hoping to scare the jewels out from their hiding.

The jewels did not leap out in fright, and she gave up and decided to go back to her room to meditate.

***

As soon as she entered her room, the two pups came rushing towards her. They were wagging their tails so hard that their entire body seemed to shake from side to side. One even toppled over in excitement.

She offered them her feet to play with as her hands were busy holding her head in despair.

The pups started worrying her ankles. She sighed and picked them up.

"My ankles are mighty worried already," she told them.

They wriggled in her grip, trying to stuff their tongues up her nose.

"Now listen here you . . . dogs? Pups? Creatures?" Lucy cuddled them closer. "Peter should give you names."

The pups gave a short bark of agreement.

"Where was I?" she mused, scratching behind a pup's ear. "Ah, yes, I was wondering who stole the jewels. I don't think the maids did it or for that matter any of the servants. Why would a servant stab the old man, steal the jewels and then continue to stagger around the manor waiting to be caught and hung? If it were me, I would have stolen the jewels, hopped into Lord Adair's balloon and taken off to a faraway land."

Here Lucy's eyes glazed, her mouth dropped open, and a bit of drool escaped the corner of her mouth as she daydreamed about holding sparkling diamonds, rubies and pearls in her hand while she floated away from Rudhall Manor on a travelling balloon.

The clouds floated by, the wind stroked her hair, and a beautiful crimson gown flowed around her. The handsome face of Lord Adair appeared in front of her, his long lashes fluttering, his dark eyes inviting. Behind him rose two giant wings made up of multiple layers of soft white feathers that shimmered in the sunlight. He beat the wings and smiled at her before pulling out a four-foot needle and piercing the balloon—

"Oof." She snapped back to the present. A pup had playfully bitten her finger a little too hard.

She nudged the animals off her lap and stood up and stretched. Once again she turned to the pups and asked, "Why would any of the servants stay after stealing the jewels? Unless they were to gain something further by staying here . . . For instance, the ingratiating butler. Hodgson knew Lord Sedley's habits well. He has been at Rudhall the longest, and if any secret passages lead in and out of Lord Sedley's room, then he would know it." She thoughtfully tapped a cheek with her finger. "What if Hodgson has stolen the jewels and is waiting to take the money left to him in the will before he bolts?"

The pups wagged their tails encouragingly.

Lucy started pacing the room, her mind leapfrogging from one thought to another. The cook Mary and her helper Rose rarely ventured out of the kitchen, while Sam came in the morning for odd jobs and left by evening. The cook had mentioned that Sam had spent the day of the murder chopping wood and had only come in for a cup of tea in the afternoon.

She sucked on her bottom lip and imagined all the servants standing in a line dressed like pirates. They all had a wooden leg, an eye patch and wore nasty sneers.

Which one, she wondered, looked the most evil?

She growled low in her throat. They all looked like blasted crooks. Each one of them looked like a high class, professional criminal. Every one of them was capable of offing not only Lord Sedley but a whole bunch of rich old men.

She gasped.

What if they were all in it together? It could be a plot masterminded over the years to do away with the lusty old aristocrat. The valet would marry Lady Sedley, and after that, it was only a matter of time before the rest of the family was killed. First, Elizabeth would be pushed off a cliff. Then, Ian shot in his empty head. And as for poor dear Peter. . .

Oh, Peter, Lucy silently wailed, the worst would be planned for you. One day, the evil servants would casually mention the circus—the circus that had recently staggered into Blackwell village.

The very same circus that had a beautiful performing lion.

They would tell you tales of how unhappy this poor lion was. They would convince you of its miserable, starved plight, and then you would cave in and buy the creature.

You would buy the lion, Peter, and then the lion would eat you up. It would eat you, Peter, bones and all. It would polish you off for breakfast, and since you are so slight . . . it wouldn't even belch. Oh, no, it wouldn't even belch . . . .

The pups whined as if reading her violent thoughts.

Lucy started and blinked back to the present.

She frowned. She was wasting time by aimlessly pacing around and concocting impossible theories. Besides, the musty closed room was dulling her senses.

With a sound of frustration, she flung open her room door.

Nothing would be gained by aimless thinking she muttered to herself as she charged down the hallway.

ANYA WYLDE

She had to act; she grumbled to the painting of a sheep wearing a white wig. The sheep, it seemed, gave an almost imperceptible nod in response.

She gasped and peered at the painting a little harder. After a moment of staring at the sheep's eyelashes to see if they moved, she gave up and decided to head towards the butler's room.

If the man had stolen the jewels, then she would find them. She would inspect every little hole, every crack and every single aberration . . . .

She found the butler's room empty of a human and ghostly presence. Pleased, she plunged straight into the task at hand. She started inspecting all the holes and the cracks and the aberrations, and it all seemed to be going rather well until the butler decided to stroll in sooner than expected.

He caught her sitting on top of his cupboard scratching at the chipped moulding on the wall with a knitting needle.

He silently pointed to her and then the floor.

Lucy dropped the knitting needle and climbed down from the cupboard with the help of a chair that she had balanced on top of a table.

"I saw a spider," she said, her eyes wide and innocent. "I was trying to squish him for you."

He crossed his arms and eyed her grimly.

"Truly," she tried again, this time adding a few helpless blinks.

He glanced at the open cupboard, the upturned vase lying on the bed and the letters scattered on the floor. His lips curled into a disbelieving snarl.

"It was a big spider," she offered half-heartedly. "Massive, in fact. Lots of legs. Ran all over the room."

He jerked his head towards the door, and she meekly departed.

Once outside, her shoulders drooped, and she miserably shuffled down the corridor towards her room. This was a terrible turn of events. She had angered her only living ally.

As she passed by the kitchen, her slipper dislodged from her foot, scattering her thoughts and bringing her to an abrupt halt. She turned to find Lord Adair holding it out for her.

"What are you doing in this part of the house, my lord?" she asked as she hopped on one foot trying to shove the slipper back in the other.

"I think it's time I learned how to cook."

"Cook? You should be finding the culprit," she exclaimed.

He leaned against the wall watching her in amusement. "Miss Trotter, you seem to be digging a very large hole for yourself. It is impressive, really."

She gave up on the shoe and shoved it in her pocket. "What do you mean?"

"You have convinced the family that you are guilty, and now it seems even downstairs, your reputation has dropped off a cliff."

She threw a surly look at him and turned to leave.

His hand shot out and caught her arm. He flipped her back around to face him. His voice was low and earnest when he said, "Stop this foolishness, Miss Trotter—"

"I have no reason to trust you," she said breathlessly. "You are Ian's friend, and you admitted you owe him your life. What if he killed his father? Would you save his neck or mine?"

She did not wait for him to reply but wrenching free from his grip hobbled away as fast as her singularly clad foot could take her.

Chapter 22

Lord Adair had been correct in his assumption that Lucy's reputation downstairs had dropped off a cliff, and a very high cliff at that.

Immediately upon her entry into the kitchen, eyes narrowed, lips twisted, cheeks flushed, and yet not a single servant looked at her directly. They either examined the roof or the floor or focused their entire concentration on the objects closest at hand.

She had never seen the cook so engrossed in an empty stew pot before, and as for the butler, why, he was glaring at the spoon as if it was his arch-enemy.

The servants had decided to give her the cut sublime and the cut infernal all at the same time, and it came as no surprise to her that her request for breakfast was ignored.

But Lucy had grown up in an orphanage and growing up in an orphanage was as good as growing up in the middle of a desert. You learned to see the brighter side of life, to turn a bad thing on its head, and no matter how sparse the basic necessities, you learned to make the best of it.

Therefore, like a desert nomad, she hardened herself against the arid looks, sharp frowns and the pooh-poohs and went where the oasis lay.

The servants were ignoring her, and the family continued to look through her. Hence, it only stood to reason that when Lucy piled her plate with a generous slice of juicy ham, hot rolls and a slab of pound cake, they would continue to ignore her presence.

The moist cake on Lucy's plate made the cook's face perform acrobatics, Rose looked like a kettle about to whistle, and as for poor Susie, why, the dear girl seemed about to weep at the sight of the large slice of ham bobbing by her hungry nose.

Lucy halted near the door, turned back around and inspected the faces in the kitchen.

The servants appeared to be out of sorts.

Lucy beamed at the sullen faces, held the plate close to her chest and rocked back and forth on her feet. "I almost forgot the tea," she remarked just as the cook placed a freshly brewed pot on a tray meant for Lady Sedley.

Lucy placed her plate next to the teapot on the tray and lifted the whole thing up.

The cook almost spluttered, and Susie's vexed fingers twitched.

Lucy sent them all another sunny smile and with a merry tune on her lips, strolled out of the kitchen.

ANYA WYLDE

No-one stopped her, though they did seem to be rethinking their strategy as to how to handle the pesky governess in future.

Once alone, Lucy's shoulders slumped, and the tray felt heavy in her grip. She gloomily made her way towards the breakfast room.

At the door, she paused. The family was eating breakfast inside. She heard the ebb and flow of conversation, the clinking of glasses and cutlery and unhappily turned around and made her way towards the library instead.

She nudged the door open with her dejected hip.

No welcoming fire burned today.

She picked at her food, sitting on the writing-table placed near the window. She stared out at the leafless trees and dried grass that shimmered like a never-ending golden carpet in the sunlight. She had never felt so alone before, not even at the orphanage. At least there she had a few friends and Miss Summer, but here—

A loud bang as someone slammed the door shut in the house made her jump. Her moping temporarily put on hold she gulped down her fourth and final cup of tea and stood up.

What she needed was to get away from the house, to gain a fresh perspective, to see the problem from all angles and to rethink what she had already thought of for the seventy-fifth time.

***

ANYA WYLDE

Lucy meandered towards the wooden bench that faced the animal house and perched her bottom upon it.

She gloomily inspected the dark, turbulent sky. The grey clouds seemed to be hurrying along as if late for critical engagement. The sun was taking an afternoon nap somewhere out of sight.

The wind suddenly sharpened and attacked her hair and the black pins holding up her bun slipped out in protest. She absently caught the pins in her hand and pocketed them.

The wind continued to whizz about racing in and out of her long hair. A strand of dark hair became so excited that it whipped her in the eye.

She wiped her watering eyes and sniffed dolefully. Her own dark locks wanted to beat her up.

After a few moments of splashing around in a pool of self-pity, she had that feeling—that strange feeling that one gets when one is being watched.

She rubbed the back of her prickling neck and ever so slightly moved her head around.

She found Spooner, the blasted Egyptian bird, eyeing her evilly.

She slowly turned her head back around. Surely things couldn't get worse than this?

Snowflakes settled on her nose mockingly.

It was one of those days where fate decided that you were a baby bird that needed to be thrown out of the nest, again and again, to test how long it took for the wings to work right.

Lucy knew how to handle such situations, having experienced plenty of them. She decided to chirp and move location. Accordingly, she carefully stood up, well aware of the evil bird and with slow, cautious steps walked towards the animal house.

She paused, wondering where to go next. The snow had started falling in earnest, and the bird had begun to hop from one foot to the other in an increasingly spirited fashion.

She eyed the animal house debating what was worse—being eaten alive by a Bengal tiger which may be living inside or freezing in the snow and then being pecked to death by a large moody bird.

She decided to take her chances with the tiger. It somehow seemed a less painful way of departing the earthly realm.

Tigers were large with sharp teeth and prominent jaws. A tiger would take a moment to gulp her down. It wouldn't hurt for long before she was blissfully dead, whereas if she lingered outside any longer, her limbs would become numb with cold.

She would freeze like an icicle unable to move, and the cruel Egyptian bird would gleefully approach her and slowly start pecking at her toes.

The bird would peck at her poor, tiny toes using its sharp beak, and inch by inch it would move upwards, leaving behind a trail of burning, raw, bloody flesh . . .

With a quick shake of her head to dispel the image, Lucy stepped into the animal house.

Her senses were immediately overwhelmed. She felt as if she had left winter behind, skipped spring and walked straight into summer.

Coos, choos, chee chees and chirps filled the air.

It took her a few moments to adjust to the cacophony. Thereafter, she was pulled towards a few giant cages filled with greenery.

She curiously peered at the strange plants inside the cage and spotted several exotic birds with brilliantly coloured feathers darting to and fro among leaves and branches.

She grasped the bars and watched the birds for a while. One particular shiny blue bird with a sleepy-looking head warmed her heart.

Delighted with her discovery, she quickly moved deeper into the old orangery wondering what else she would find.

She could hear a fountain tinkling somewhere in the room. She started making her way towards the source of the tinkling water stopping now and then to inspect her immediate surroundings.

She spied mysterious baskets placed on top of high shelves and gaped at carved statues of Roman and Greek gods that stood frozen amongst unfamiliar plants.

Further down some pigs snorted a greeting at her, and her nose wrinkled at the heavy animal scent lacing the air.

She soon found herself pulling at the edges of her collar. It was warm inside. It was also wonderful. She regretted not visiting before.

She strolled from cage to cage, at times stopping to mimic the animal sounds. She chirruped back at the birds, croaked at the toads and chittered along with the squirrels.

The animals pranced, sang and whooped as if greeting an esteemed guest. She felt special, like a jungle queen being welcomed home by her relatives. Every furry face that she passed seemed to be smiling and nodding at her. Even the birds seemed to be watching her with a happy twinkle in their eyes.

She sighed with contentment, and a feeling of tranquil peace invaded her agitated soul.

The worries of the last few days melted away, and a few primitive emotions started awakening within her. It was as if her soul remembered that she was no different from the animals.

In fact, her soul insisted that she was a wild creature.

Animals drank and slept and played and sang. They dined on leaves, fruits and other creatures smaller than themselves . . . and so did she. Had she not enjoyed chewing on a juicy chicken, the head of an artichoke or a sprig of mint?

And it wasn't long before she could no longer recall what separated her from the birds, squirrels and toads.

She had become one with the animals.

Her oneness was so complete that when a large yellow snake hissed at her through a hole in a wooden box, she hissed back.

It was, indeed, a spiritual moment. She felt almost enlightened at that point in her young life.

Soon she arrived at a cage where a beautiful peacock stood with his wings spread. She dared to inch closer and closer to the cage, her eyes locked on the brilliant colours in his wings that sparkled like a thousand colourful jewels. Her nose inched through the bars.

The peacock charged.

She reeled back swiftly and hopped a good few feet away from the cage, her hand grasping her brave little nose.

After that, her love for nature dimmed a little. She decided to appreciate it from afar and not become a part of it.

With such philosophical thoughts plodding along in her mind, she walked towards the pond and found tiny colourful fish whizzing about.

Further down, she found white mice, and still further, balls of pearly wool and old cloth stuffed in brown paper bags. She had almost walked away from it when a soft mewing alerted her. The wool turned out to be adorable little kittens, the sort she had only ever seen in watercolours before.

As her senses adjusted to the chaos, she started noticing signs of repair. The glass in the windows had been replaced in a few places with planks of wood—perhaps to save tax— a beam was broken, statues chipped and faded, and the shelves and the green leaves were covered with a layer of dirt and dust.

She discovered a chicken coup right at the back. She smiled at the sight of a few fat hens sitting in a neat little row.

The hens eyed her warily.

She wondered if they had laid any eggs. She made clucking sounds hoping one of the birds would stand up and let her inspect.

The hens continued to sit tight, and their wariness increased.

She clucked at a higher pitch. The stubborn birds, she thought annoyed, might as well be guarding precious stones the way they were attached to the ground refusing to budge.

A cluck froze in her throat as her mind leapt from dot to dot.

What if the thief had kept the jewels under the hens? The hens were right at the back and concealed from view. No one came to the animal house, and Peter was so absent-minded that if he saw the jewels, he would forget about them the next moment.

She eyed the hens speculatively. Were the jewels under their bellies? Were they warming their eggs along with gold nuggets and diamond necklaces?

There was only one way to find out.

"Up, up, up," she coaxed them.

They cocked their heads to the left.

"Hurr-hurr, gack-gack, BOO!" she tried to scare them.

They cocked their heads to the right.

"Phooey- phooey, cluck-cluck, chick- chick," she said, trying to speak what she hoped was chicken language.

They squawked threateningly.

She scurried back a foot and scratched her head. She was afraid of getting too close to the birds, let alone lift them off the eggs . . . How did Peter teach his pets to behave?

At his one command, she had seen the animals behave in the most amazing ways. The pups knew how to roll over and sit quietly. Palmer ate with a spoon and was almost human in his understanding whenever Peter spoke to him. Even Spinoza left her bonnet alone if ordered by him.

She recalled Palmer mimicking Peter in the morning room once. Peter would open a book and close it, and the baboon would do the same. Peter had clapped his hands and Palmer had copied him, though a touch more enthusiastically.

What if she, too, showed the hens what she wanted them to do? Would they understand?

Might as well take a stab at it, she thought, and fetched a few smooth stones and placed them on the ground. She lifted her dress, squatted over the stones and peered at the hens wondering if they were watching.

They were.

Lucy suddenly sprang up and leapt to the side, triumphantly revealing the stones.

The hens kept sitting, and if anything, they now looked sulky.

Lucy frowned and squatted over the stones again. "Now look here, hens. I am sitting on my eggs. Cluck, cluck, cluck, and I am warming them now. Mmm, nice and warm. Now I pull up my skirts, jump to the side and voila! Here are the eggs . . . Come, now, your turn. Down we go, cluck cluck cluck . . . Now, we are warming the eggs, warming the eggs," Here she whistled an encouraging tune, "and then you spring aside and the eggs are revealed!"

A gasp behind her made her freeze mid squat. She slowly turned around to find Elizabeth, Peer, Lady Sedley, Ian and Lord Adair gaping at her.

She let her skirts drop.

"We came to see the kittens," Peter mumbled. "Did we . . . err . . . disturb you in your . . . err . . . ." He closed his mouth uncertain as to how to complete that sentence.

Lucy looked around wide-eyed and then decided to scoot. Nothing could explain what she had been trying to do.

She quickly walked past the group and overheard Elizabeth mummer to Lord Adair, "I told you the girl was loony. She has to be the murderer."

Chapter 23

A nomad in a desert would not have moped around and wasted tears in a land that is parched. No, a true nomad would have continued to wander in the blazing heat with hot sand under blistering feet searching and occasionally ripping apart cacti for a drink, hopping over poisonous lizards, snakes and other gruesome stuff.

Lucy was once again that hardened nomad. She wouldn't give up. No, sir, she was going to shuffle through the sand, bake in the blazing sun and continue onward to safety.

Hence, twenty minutes after the chicken fiasco, she bounced back up and snuck into the upstairs study, the same room where the jewels had been hidden in the priest hole.

She entered the room and swiftly cast a look around. It looked the same as usual. The large desk sat looking bored in one corner, the leather-covered books lining the tall shelves were busy gathering dust, and the long green sofa contemplatively peered out of the window.

She wilted. All she could see for miles was never-ending sand and not a drop of water.

The trouble was that she didn't know where to begin. All her efforts until now had been not just hopeless but also disastrous.

A magazine partially jutting out of the bookshelf caught her eye.

She walked over and read the black scrawl on the binding. It was titled *The Anti-Jacobin Review*. She pulled it out and immediately spotted the priest hole hidden behind it.

She took out a few more books to see the priest hole better. It was a hollowed-out space carved inside the stone wall and concealed behind several dull tomes. It would have comfortably hidden a three-foot, four-inch priest and no more.

The metal safe which should have been in the priest hole was missing.

She wasn't surprised. Lord Adair must have advised the family to move the safe to a more secret location.

She stuck her hand inside the priest hole and ran her sensitive fingers along the sides, looking for a missed clue or a hidden catch.

She wondered as she searched if anyone had ever needed to squish themselves into such a small space, and if they had, then how long had it taken them to straighten out their limbs after coming back out into the world.

It wasn't long before she realised that the blasted hole was empty with nary a clue nor a catch.

Her bottom lip started trembling, and she bit it hard to make it behave.

She carefully replaced the books making sure that The *Anti-Jacobin Review* was jutting out in the exact same way as it had done before. Thereafter, she squared her shoulders like a sergeant major and went and sat at Lord Sedley's large desk—not the live Lord Sedley but the dead one—who was probably dining somewhere in hell at the moment.

She frowned as a vision of the late Lord Sedley sitting on red velvet chair rose up unbidden in her mind's eye. She imagined him bouncing in his seat, clapping his hands together as he tried to kill mosquitoes and flies. Surely hell had plenty of insects considering how warm it was . . . .

She leaned back in her seat and rolled a quill between her palms. A vague idea was forming at the back of her head. An idea not related to Lord Sedley chasing after lady demons—if there were such things—but the idea that she should glue herself to Elizabeth for a while.

If Peter and Lady Sedley were innocent, then her biggest suspect immediately became Elizabeth.

Ian could have done it, but to finish off the deed with such finesse was beyond his abilities. Not that she was in any hurry to cross the blasted man off the list, but for the moment, she wanted to focus on his sister.

The door creaked as someone pushed it open, and Lucy immediately slipped under the desk.

It was as if Lucy had used the power of her mind to yank the person she needed to shadow closer to herself, for right then Elizabeth sashayed into the room.

Lucy nervously clutched her skirts and peeked from the side of the solid rosewood desk. The legs of the desk, she noted, were beautifully carved but dusty. Stifling a sneeze, her pupils tracked Elizabeth around the room.

Elizabeth's swayed over to the books.

Lucy, who could only see Elizabeth's narrow back draped in black satin, decided that the hard shoulders were drooping thoughtfully, the fingertips were tracing the titles too quickly, and her head was tilting at an angle as if carrying some heavy burden hidden inside the tightly wound up bun.

Elizabeth suddenly slapped the wooden case making Lucy jump and turned away with a mew of frustration. She looked around distractedly and froze when she caught sight of the large Venetian mirror hanging over the fireplace. It seemed as if her reflection had arrested her, and she moved closer to the mirror.

Lucy watched Elizabeth's reflection as it squinted its dark eyes and tilted its head. She thought Elizabeth looked beautiful, like a perfectly carved ice sculpture clad in black silk and with a head full of thick, dark golden hair.

But Elizabeth, it seemed, did not like what she saw reflected in the mirror, for she further narrowed her eyes, and the corner of her mouth turned down. A finger went up to rub an obnoxious freckle that had dared to appear on her cheek. The freckle stayed put, and after a moment, she gave up and let her hand fall. Next, she straightened her shoulders, smoothed back her hair and smiled at herself.

Lucy's lips quirked along with the reflection.

Elizabeth's nose was now the point of interest. It seemed she thought it was too large, for she sucked in a deep breath forcing her nose to pinch in response. Keeping her nostrils squeezed together, she moved her head from side to side, inspecting her profile. Finally, she thrust her lips out and pouted.

Apparently satisfied with what she saw she relaxed her face and departed with quick, efficient steps.

Lucy emerged from behind the desk and walked over to the door. She stuck her head out and looked up and down the corridor.

No one was around.

Pleased, she stuck her head back in and walked over to the oval mirror.

The girl who looked back at her was nothing like Elizabeth. Her hair was not smooth but pulled up in a messy bun. Long wavy tresses floated about her heart-shaped face, the large brown eyes were frightened and the lips too full and rebellious.

Lucy took a deep breath and sucked in her nostrils just as she had seen Elizabeth do. But her nostrils didn't seem to stick together like Elizabeth's had.

She tried harder, attempting to make her nose look slimmer. She sucked, pouted and moved her head to see her profile.

It didn't work. Her nose remained tilted up and considerably bigger than Elizabeth's delicate one.

She exhaled sharply annoyed at the foolishness that had distracted her. A bit of snot escaped her nostrils and dangled dangerously near her upper lip.

"Handkerchief?"

She squealed and whirled around in shock.

A hand was waving a white handkerchief at her from one end of the olive green sofa that sat facing the window.

Mortified, Lucy quickly wiped her nose on her own grey handkerchief and walked up to the couch.

An amused Lord Adair was lying full length on it. He held a twinkling crystal glass filled with an amber liquid in one relaxed grip, and an open book lay upside down on his chest.

His position had hidden him from her view, but the room was clearly reflected in the windowpane making it clear that he had watched her every move.

Lucy bobbed a curtsy. "I didn't see you, my lord."

He smiled and went back to reading his book.

ANYA WYLDE

She hesitated, her eyes on his splendid form decorating the sofa. She hadn't spoken to a human being in hours and hours. . . .

"What are you reading?" she asked tentatively.

"Poems by a misunderstood poet called Philbert Woodbead," he said turning a page.

"I didn't think you were the sort to enjoy poetry."

"And I, Miss Trotter, thought that by now you would be bobbing along in the river of self-pity," he said, his eyes not leaving the book.

"Well, I am not," she replied forcefully. "In fact, I am cheerful enough. Bright as a singing grasshopper."

"Remarkable," he said, letting the book fall back on his muscular chest. "I have unravelled all the mysteries that this manor could possibly hold, and yet I am confounded as to why you are not beating your head on the cushion repeatedly and wailing like a banshee. You don't appear to be loony . . . ." He trailed off.

He had asked her this before, but today he was eyeing her differently, not in a condescending or indulgent way but curiously as if he truly wanted to know.

And since she had nothing better to do, she decided to tell him.

"Close your eyes," she said as she moved around the couch to face him.

He promptly did as he was told.

ANYA WYLDE

The sun was setting, and the red glow filtered through the gap in the curtain to fall on his peaceful face. His hands were folded together on his stomach, and his ankles crossed.

"Imagine the world is dark and stars are glittering in the sky," she said softly. A part of her wondered at his calm obedience.

He nodded slightly, his eyes still tightly shut.

"In the night sky," her voice trembled, "are three stars standing together in a row. Those stars are the reason I don't cry, my lord."

His eyes flew open, and understanding laced his expression.

She continued speaking, perhaps because it was easier to share the deepest part of your soul with a stranger. "They are my parents and the sibling I never had. The stars, I mean. Miss Summer had told me when I was young that my parents died and became stars. She said that I was lucky . . . because from now on they would cast their brilliant light on me. A light that would keep me safe from demons and monsters, chase away my nightmares and let nothing harmful happen to me."

"You believed her?"

"I didn't at first, but over the years, girls in the orphanage dropped off like flies because of disease, want or despair. The darkness evaded me. I remained sane and healthy, and I learned to have faith. Faith in those stars and that they were protecting me and will continue to protect me forever."

He masked his expression, his lids falling to shield his dark eyes.

"Everything will be all right," she said in a small voice.

"I will make sure it is," he replied gently.

She looked at him then, and for the first time in her life, a tiny, tiny seed of trust for a man wormed its way into her heart and buried in deep.

He ignored her after that and picking up the book started reading once again.

Chapter 24

"I will make sure it is," Lucy mimicked Lord Adair's words with a grimace. In the light of the day, they sounded hollow.

Mere platitudes.

And besides, how in the world was he supposed to help her if he spent his time reading poetry, standing on one leg— and she had even caught him dancing with the cook. What in the world was he doing romancing the kitchen staff she couldn't say.

What she could say was that the man was an utter loon and undependable.

Which was why she had once again taken charge of her destiny and decided to slither across the floor and enter Elizabeth's rooms to look for the jewels.

The slithering went well. She entered the room without being caught.

It was a largish room.

The walls were papered blue, patterned with pretty little white flowers, the pillows and cushions were sapphire hued, while the carpet was a sort of dull grey-blue.

It was a becoming colour for a carpet. As for the ceiling, it was a light azure mimicking a cloudless sky.

Even the vase on the side table and the giant mirror above the dressing table were copper tinged with blue.

In short, it was all very blue.

And it all flowed along very nicely with Lucy's blue thoughts. Pleased, she slipped into the room like a freshly oiled latch.

The room was devoid of any living occupants.

She moved further into the room.

Her heart gave a sudden hop of fear.

The room was devoid of living occupants but was it, she wondered, empty of the dead?

Her reason for being suspicious was the tall wooden door on her right. This tall wooden door had a gap at the bottom, and through that gap, a haze of mist was seeping out.

Was this mist, Aunt Sedley?

Lucy opened her mouth to ask and then closed it again. What if it wasn't aunt Sedley? What if it was some other ghost?

At that moment, she realised something critical . . .

Ghosts were like dogs.

She expanded on that thought. If you knew the dog, then you wouldn't be frightened, but if you didn't know the dog, then it was best to be wary. Which was why she decided to be wary of this new ghostly mist.

Another frightening thought slammed into her ribs as the scent of charred paper meandered over to her nose.

What if it wasn't a ghost at all—her heart started beating rapidly—but smoke bellowing out of from below the closet door?

"Fire!" Lucy let out a war cry.

Amid a life-threatening situation, great men have been known to baulk, but not Lucy. No, she was proud of how steady her fingers were and how clearly her mind was functioning.

Swiftly she scanned the contents in the room and spotted the ewer by the window filled with icy water.

She tilted her body at a sixty-degree angle and launched herself across the room.

She landed safely and grabbed the ewer with a firm, brave hand.

A deep breath later, she flew back towards the closet, wrenched open the door and flung the water inside.

When the frightened haze disappeared from her vision, she spotted an even more terrifying sight. . .

A dripping Elizabeth was sitting on a red velvet stool near a dressing table with a drenched book in one hand and a drooping cigar in the other.

"You were smoking," Lucy stammered in horror. "I thought . . . fire . . . Goodbye."

***

ANYA WYLDE

That last incident had admittedly shaken Lucy. Every single strand of hair on her head quivered whenever she thought of the red-eyed, soaking Elizabeth.

It was bound to happen. The hope in her heart had to, at some point, duck its head back into its shell like a frightened turtle. Hence, she crept around the manor for the rest of the day, avoiding all human contact.

Nighttime, however, was a different story. The house was asleep, her three favourite courage inducing stars were shining and the fat moon was dangling in the sky.

The trouble was that it was dark and, unfortunately, she was not an owl or a firefly or a fruit-eating bat. She needed a candle if she wanted to continue hunting for the jewels.

She nervously sucked on a dry tongue. She didn't mind lighting a candle and letting it sit on a table far from her ignitable self, but to actually hold one for an extended period?

Her hand started trembling. What if she tripped and the candle slipped from her fingers, rolled across the floor and reached the curtains, all before she had picked herself up.

She could potentially set the house ablaze.

She didn't want Lord Adair to go up in flames simply because she had tripped. He was too handsome. It would be sheer injustice if a man like him departed this world without first producing beautiful children.

But she couldn't very well flounder around in the dark either, hoping her small paws would miraculously land on a bag of jewels.

The pugs barked for attention. In spite of the trouble they had got her into with Lady Sedley, she had once again sneaked them up the stairs for a cuddle. They were irresistible.

"Do you think I can hold on to a candle for one night? Or perhaps two?" she asked the animals.

They licked her face.

She grimaced. "Comforting to see you have complete confidence in me."

Another lick had her giggling.

"Ugh, you smell rotten. Fine, I shall take the plunge. Dip my toes in frigid waters, charge towards the fight and slay the enemy. I shall survive the holding of the candle," she promised them.

"Scared of a candle?" Aunt Sedley asked, sailing into the room.

The room immediately turned cold. The pillows started inflating and deflating, while the quilt raced about all over the bed.

The pups hid under Lucy's skirts. She stroked their heads comfortingly. "You have left your hair undone," she commented.

"Mr Brown prefers it this way," Aunt Sedley replied shyly.

"Ah."

"I glow in the dark," Aunt Sedley said after a moment. She was floating on her back, her hands moving as if she was swimming in mid-air.

"Hmm," Lucy replied. She detached herself from the pugs who had latched onto her skirts with their teeth and went to look for the tinder box.

"I could light your path. You wouldn't need a candle."

Lucy jerked her head in the spirit's direction, almost hurting the muscles in her neck. "Would you truly do that for me?"

"I would, but I can't. I am going with Mr Brown for a celebration."

Lucy went back to hunting for the box. "What are you celebrating?"

"His sister just died. It is her funeral."

"Oh, I am so sorry."

"Don't be. It is a happy occasion. He is very fond of his sister, and now he will have her back in his . . . death."

"In his death?"

"I was going to say life, but changed it to death because . . . ." Aunt Sedley trailed off.

Lucy cleared her throat, "Yes, well . . . Congratulations."

"Thank you."

"And the hairdo looks lovely on you."

The ghost simpered.

Lucy continued, "I have nothing important to report."

"Eh?"

"About the murder."

"Oh, yes . . . Well, I will be back, and you can tell me all about it," Aunt Sedley said distractedly. Her limbs were already fading.

"Goodbye," Lucy curtseyed.

Aunt Sedley waggled her fingers in response. Her voice echoed around the room, "I will be back. I promise next time I will try and help you, Miss Trotter. I will be your firefly. . . firefly . . . firefly. . . ."

"No, she won't," Lucy muttered to the pups. "Lazy lump of—"

"I heard that," Aunt Sedley's faraway voice growled.

"I am sorry," Lucy yelled back.

The ding dong of a grandfather clock was all she got in reply.

***

Around two in the morning, Lucy's part frightened part hopeful ear emerged from her room and weaved its way around the manor. The candle periodically trembled in her grasp, and the hot wax dripped onto the back of her hand, making her jump and stifle a squeal.

Her ear attached itself to various doors on its way to Elizabeth's room, straining to hear a single sound.

Her ear was disappointed until it plastered itself against Lady Sedley's gleaming oak door.

A hint of sound, a shuffle . . . Was someone speaking?

Lucy moved her nervous toes closer to the door, her ear now wholly flattened against the wood.

Someone was speaking. If only she could hear the words . . . Shifting even closer, she brought her palms up to cup her ear.

Did someone say, governess?

Her body tilted and leaned heavily against the door; the door that belonged to Lady Sedley's room, the door that had not been locked, the door that could not, even if it wanted to, hold an entire human body resting against itself.

It had to happen, and nothing in the world could have stopped it. No physics, no magical light from the stars, no quick thinking acrobatics could have stopped Lucy from tumbling into the room at that point.

From beneath naughty sheets, the valet and Lady Sedley eyed her sprawled form in disgust.

Lucy scrambled up and dusted her skirt. "Where am I?" she asked after a tense moment.

Lady Sedley growled in warning.

"Egad." Lucy fluttered her lashes at the couple on the bed. "I am in your room . . . How? . . . I don't know what happened. I was asleep on my bed . . . Did you bring me here?"

The valet raised a disbelieving eyebrow.

Lucy widened her eyes. "If you didn't bring me here, then . . . Oh, I must have walked in my sleep. I often do this sort of thing . . . stroll around at night. It comes on like a fit, particularly on moonless nights."

"If what you say is true, then I," Lady Sedley snorted, "am a moulting duck."

"Quack, quack?" Lucy queried.

Lady Sedley narrowed her eye s. "If I catch you lurking upstairs, prowling in the night or eavesdropping ever again, then you, Miss Lucy Anne Trotter, will be sleeping in the stables."

Lucy quietly slinked away.

***

One would think that after so many violent disruptions and tragic ends of complex plans, Lucy would give up. Anyone would have, and anyone should have for the sake of other people's health and safety, but consider Lucy's position.

She was a suspect in a murder case. She was alone with not a single soul to call her own. She had limited time within which she had to prove her innocence and save her slim, pretty neck and admirable earlobes.

Those earlobes deserved to live.

And was being caught snooping, drenching a fellow human with icy water or playing with the chickens worse than murder and theft? She had already been charged with the worst, and these small hiccups where she tumbled into other peoples' rooms were not significant.

What was important was to keep her heart beating, her lungs functioning and the livers and kidneys continuing to do what they were supposed to be doing. She couldn't stop hunting for clues.

That would be foolish.

She would keep trying until she found the jewels and the murderer unless she was packed off to Bedlam.

Feeling better after this short discussion in her head, Lucy meandered towards the upstairs study. She wanted to recreate how a thief could have stolen the jewels.

Perhaps he had left some clues that had been missed by others near the crime scene.

It is said that when faced with bad luck once, become a hedgehog. Retreat into your spiny shell and do not emerge until misfortune hobbles away with the moon.

And if it is not a saying, then it should be because if it had been said, then Lucy would have heard it, and if she had heard it, then she wouldn't have tested her luck.

Lucy pushed open the door of the library, and lousy luck eyed her like a fly rubbing its hands together in glee sitting atop a basket of overripe fruit.

Ian was sitting at the desk, trying his best to finish off his late father's bottles of wine and whiskey.

He leered at her. "Come to keep me company, eh?"

"Mr Sedley. I am sorry, I didn't mean to disturb you," Lucy said, inching back towards the door.

For a sozzled creature, Ian moved mighty quickly. He was beside her in a flash. "Not at all. It is a delight to see you staggering in here on such a cold night. An ant that has come sniffing for bits of leftover dinner . . . me being the dinner."

"I am not hungry," Lucy protested, her feet ever so slowly moving backwards.

"Have a nibble. You will find that you are starving," he said, catching her around the waist.

Lucy eyed his hairy chin, yellow teeth and sharp nose in horror.

She inhaled sharply and was treated to a blast of sour whisky fumes emanating from his mouth. She cursed and twisted in his grip.

He smirked.

She gripped his hair and tried to yank it with all her might. His hair was oilier than usual. The greasy strands slipped right through her fingers.

Lucy had a frightening thought. She was about to be ruined forever.

"I told you I will back to help you," the ghost of Aunt Sedley remarked irritably.

The temperature immediately plummeted and the room chilled at the arrival of the spirit. The cushions gave a nervous twitch, and the drapes shivered.

Aunt Sedley crossed her arms and scowled at Lucy. "You need to learn how to trust people. You hurt my feelings, and don't you dare mention my lack of heart or the fact that I said people and not spirits or spiritoo . . . I see we are short on time. Ian getting frisky, is he? Watch his finger! Now, this is what you must do . . . ."

Sometime later, Elizabeth, Lord Adair and a sleepy Peter raced into the library.

"What happened? I heard a scream," Elizabeth asked, staring at Lucy.

Lucy stood, wringing her hands. Her hair was cascading down her shoulders, part of her sleeve was ripped off, and a button swung loose from a single thread in her bodice.

"Was it one of the animals? It sounded like my pig, Mr Bacon," Peter asked worriedly.

Lucy bit her lip. "I had to. He wouldn't let go. He wanted me to nibble him, and honestly, he smelled so foul I couldn't bear it any longer—"

"Good lord, she has killed my brother," Elizabeth screeched staring at the ground behind Lucy.

Lord Adair went and nudged Ian with his boot.

Ian moaned.

"He is alive, merely dazed," Lord Adair observed. He bent down and further inspected the damage. He whistled in appreciation. "Remarkable job with the rope. You have tied him up well."

ANYA WYLDE

Lucy straightened up in pleasure.

"Where did you get the rope?" Elizabeth asked, her nostrils flaring in disapproval.

"I carry one at all times," Lucy replied demurely.

"He has been stabbed with what looks like hairpins," Lord Adair said. "Painful but not lethal. I doubt he will dare to misbehave with a woman again."

"He won't," Lucy said with a glint in her eye.

"He has a doorknob stuck between his—" Lord Adair's lips pressed together.

"Yes, well, I know nothing about that," Lucy said primly.

Aunt Sedley gave a ghostly chuckle.

"And a piece of chalk up his left nostril," Lord Adair continued after an uncomfortable pause.

Lucy pretended not to hear him this time.

Aunt Sedley patted Lucy on the back for a job well done. The transparent hand merely passed through her ribcage a few times, but Lucy understood the intent and appreciated it for what it was.

Lord Adair untied Ian, removed the chalk and left the doorknob.

"I am going to bed." Elizabeth snapped.

Lord Adair flicked a glance at her without moving his head.

Elizabeth immediately smoothed her face and spoke in a helpless, fluttery sort of voice, "I am tired, Lord Adair, and you must be too. Don't worry about Ian. Peter can take care of him."

Peter yawned and pulled off one of his robes—he had been wearing two for some odd reason—and lobbed it at Ian's drunken chest. Next, he picked up a book and jammed it under Ian's head.

After that, everyone stared at Ian on the floor for a moment and then with a satisfactory nod departed for bed.

Chapter 25

"Miss Trotter," Lord Adair said, catching her on the way to the servants' rooms.

She paused and lifted her chin defiantly.

"Leave the investigations to me."

She kicked a little ornate side table placed against the wall."I wonder why Lady Sedley keeps such an ugly piece of furniture."

"Do not," he said sternly, "try and distract me with inanities."

"No, truly, why does she keep this. Look at it. I have never seen a more hideous object in my life."

"Miss Trotter—"

"It is covered in pink leather—"

"It is brown, but—"

"No, look. The brown is the dirt accumulated over the years. It is, in fact, pink. I spilt a bit of tea on it the other day and here ... you can see the flesh colour glowing through."

He shuddered and looked away. "It must have been restored at a later stage. It is about a hundred years old—"

"Ugh! Why the devil does she keep such old things?"

"It is an antique piece—"

"My dress is ten years old. Is it antique?"

"No. It is appalling, though."

"Who determines what is an antique, and what is not?"

"Old objects have a story to tell or are nostalgic pieces—"

"Who determines which story is important and which is not? If my dress could speak, it would entertain you with plenty of tales—"

"Miss Trotter."

"Yes?" she asked coyly.

"Behave."

She kicked the table.

"Stop it. I told you it is a hundred years old. It is fragile. Besides, young ladies shouldn't go around kicking things. It is not done."

"Not done? Now you sound like an antique piece." She peeked at him from underneath her lashes and once again kicked the table.

His lips pursed in disapproval.

"I am sorry," she said, feeling guilty. "I am not sure why I did that. It was almost as if an invisible imp grasped my foot and threw it at the table."

"I see."

"You do?" she asked in wonder. "I don't see how you could, though, because I said it and I don't see what I said. Then how could you see it? Let me explain more clearly—"

"Leave the investigations to me," he interrupted.

"You already said that," she told her feet.

"Look at me," he ordered.

She slowly lifted her chin, crossed her eyes and stuck her tongue out.

"I am losing patience," he said softly, "and that, my dear, is a rare thing."

The presence of Aunt Sedley's ghost usually sucked all the warmth out of a room, but Lord Adair seemed to have the opposite effect.

She started feeling feverish, and his warning tone had raised the temperature a few more degrees.

The hallway felt narrower, the ceiling lower and the air around them seemed to tense like tightly pulled violin strings.

All thoughts of mischief fled from her mind.

"You are one of them," she said, jerking her head towards the rooms above.

"Miss Trotter, I admit it was amusing watching you hop around aimlessly—"

She stifled a yawn and let the words roll off her back. He had a lovely deep dark voice. She could stand here and listen to him forever swaying to and fro, to and fro, and sometimes fro and to . . . .

He lifted the candle closer to himself, and the dim yellow light was awfully flattering. His lips were moving, and his hair shimmering. The muscles in his neck were taught, and the woody scent of him engulfed her senses.

Lord Adair continued to speak passionately. "You have been hopping about disguised as foliage. You have been caught hiding under Lady Sedley's bed, prowling around the manor at night, beaten up Mr Sedley and then tied him up—"

Lucy tilted her head and frowned. He had a nose, two eyes and lips, and yet somehow every one of those features was so delectable in Lord Adair while ordinary in others.

"Stuck pins all over him, doing devil knows what with the hens—"

Lucy sighed. It was a waste . . . He really should marry and produce beautiful children. It was his duty to do so . . .

"So you will leave the investigations to me from now on. The wager is off. You are digging yourself into a larger and larger hole. It will become impossible for me t—"

Burnt Lamb chops were what an ordinary man was compared to him. While Lord Adair was a feast of spun sugar, mashed turnip, almond pudding, tender veal, vibrant olives, powdered rump with greens, fricassee of calf's feet, turkey in chestnut sauce . . .

"I hope you understand, Miss Trotter, how dangerous—"

He was wearing a robe again. A long silk black robe which rustled sensuously every time he moved his hands to make a point. It made him appear more thrilling, exciting and magnificent . . .

A sudden thought struck Lucy. It snuck past her impassioned exploration of Lord Adair's good looks and rang for attention like a discordant bell.

Why, the discordant bell jingled, had Elizabeth been dressed at this hour? Everyone else had arrived wearing robes.

"Are you listening to me, Miss Trotter? Miss Trotter?" Lord Adair asked, shaking her arm.

Lucy blinked. "Yes, what you say is true." She blurted out the first thing that came to her head.

"It is?"

"Yes," she nodded more confidently.

"What is true?"

"I shouldn't have tied him up."

Lord Adair closed his eyes, and before Lucy could once again get lost in admiring his eyelashes, he opened them again. "Go to bed, Miss Trotter. We will have this conversation tomorrow."

Lucy curtsied and departed with a final lustful look at his beautifully shaped nostrils.

"Doxie," Aunt Sedley observed bobbing after her.

Chapter 26

"Foolish woman," Rose, the cook's aide, muttered.

Lucy ignored her.

"Maykes me mad as de' devils," Rose growled, looking sideways at Lucy. "Murdherir, dief, no yentleman's otter."

Lucy slurped her tea loudly.

Rose attacked the dough with a rolling pin. "By Got, 'nother choo an I vill bite de nose."

Lucy understood the part about biting off the nose clearly enough to hurriedly leave the warm kitchen.

Her heart felt like it had abandoned its snug home in the ribcage and crawled down to her toes. In other words, she was gloomy and in no mood to match wits with Lady Sedley who would have by now discovered Ian asleep on the library floor complete with battle wounds.

Wrapping two shawls around her desperately unhappy shoulders and covering the plump bun drooping at the nape of her neck with a brown woollen scarf, she escaped outside and headed towards her favourite bench.

It had snowed again last night, but she failed to appreciate the white landscape glittering like an enchanted realm in the sunlight.

Her cheeks hurt from the cold, her eyes and nose were watering, and her heart was trying to wriggle out of her toenails.

And her heart did shoot out of her big left toe when she spotted Spooner blocking her path.

The Egyptian crane seemed to be struggling with an old scarlet sweater tied around her neck. The long-legged bird, weighing a little over ten pounds and sporting an impressive wingspan, paused in the act of pecking at the offending garment as Lucy's foot crunched on a fresh pile of snow.

The muscles in Spooner's lengthy neck moved, and the bird tilted its head to shoot a cool look at Lucy from the corner of her eyes.

Lucy eyed the bird warily.

For the next few minutes, the bird and Lucy stared at one another. The wind urgently rustled leaves, the sun shone worriedly and snow melted under a human and bird's feet

Lucy's lashes started quivering, but before she could blink, Spooner broke eye contact and spread her clipped wings, thrust her chest out and took a step forward.

Lucy's heart reeled back through her toenail, raced up her leg and once again found its home in the rib cage where it started hammering with all its might.

Spooner flapped her wings and let out a loud trumpeting sound-making Lucy leap a foot into the air, spin around and run like the devil was snapping at her heels.

"Miss Trotter," Lord Adair called out.

"Bloody blooming bird," Lucy yelled back.

"Did you just call me a blooming bird?" Lord Adair asked taken aback.

Lucy had no breath left to explain. She was too busy trying to escape the Egyptian crane.

"Miss Trotter, stop right this minute," Lord Adair ordered ambling up to her.

"Behind you," Lucy gasped.

A few seconds of brief silence ensued after which Lord Adair started running faster than Lucy and soon overtook her.

Lucy jealously watched his long legs cover ground.

"Bloody blooming bird is right," he growled as he gestured for her to follow him.

Lucy followed for she had no other plan than to aimlessly keep running until either the bird or she gave up.

Lord Adair abandoned the main path and instead leapt over a leafless bush and charged towards a clump of trees.

Lucy wondered if he was taking them towards the stables by cutting across the garden.

He veered left, ducked under a low branch and with an impatient glance back at her, sprinted onwards.

She frowned, her boots sinking into the wet mud and snow. The stables were on the right. Where was Lord Adair heading?

The sound of flapping wings silenced all thoughts and she accelerated, her eyes glued to Lord Adair's blue woollen coat warming his admirable back.

Up ahead, another group of tall, leafy trees were packed together. He led her through the clustered barks, and she was amazed to find a large building hidden behind the trees.

She had a brief sense of a square structure covered in ivy before she dashed inside and Lord Adair slammed the door closed behind them.

They both sagged against the door in relief. They were safe from Spooner for the moment.

When Lucy finally caught her breath, she looked around in bafflement. She had been living at Rudhall for over three months and never known this place existed. How had Lord Adair discovered it?

The heavy draping of ivy on the exterior and the trees guarding the place in the front blocked out most of the sunlight. It looked like an abandoned orangery or a hothouse.

Wood replaced parts that should have been covered with glass, and bars of light streamed in between the slats to illuminate broken pots, strange plants and beautifully carved pillars.

Her foot touched something on the ground, and she almost screamed at the frozen face staring up at her. It was a statue of a man with a bewitching face and damaged hands.

Her eyes adjusted to the dim light, and she noticed an odd golden glow coming from the middle of the orangery.

Lord Adair, too, seemed to have noticed it for he put a finger to his lips and quietly led her towards the light.

They crept closer and found two empty iron chairs placed around a dark ornate table.

But it was the lit lamp and the glowing cigar lying abandoned on an ashtray, its smoke still curling out and disappearing into the damp air, that made Lucy stifle a gasp.

Lord Adair took one look at the burning cigar and pulled her behind an upright statue of Dionysus.

She nodded in understanding before he could gesture her to stay quiet. Someone was using this place as a hideout or a secret meeting place and that someone could be still around.

He gave her a pleased smile before turning his attention back to the table.

Lord Adair's quick thinking worked in their favour. Whoever had been smoking that cigar returned the moment Lucy had ducked her head out of sight.

"Digby," a familiar husky voice called out.

"Don't call me that," the valet snapped.

"Well, then, Richard, you should have chosen a better name," Elizabeth replied equally irritably.

Lucy's eyebrow shot up in shock. What the devil? The valet was meant to be having an affair with Lady Sedley. Everyone knew that, so what was he doing here with Elizabeth?

"I am worried," the valet was saying. He curled his fingers around the back of the chair and continued, "I only stole the jewels. I never dreamt the old man would be offed the next day. We have to get rid of the jewels, Lizzy, or Adair is going to think I did it."

Elizabeth lit a cigarette and took a long, thoughtful pull. She handed it to the valet and spoke with smoke escaping her nostrils. "It took us six whole months of planning the theft. No one would have missed the jewels." She turned away from the valet and asked in a different tone, "You did not kill him? He may have guessed your intentions and . . . Oh, don't be angry, my dearest pineapple. I am merely speculating, and even if you had done it, I would stand by you. I held no love for my father, you know that. He had been cruel to all of us and—"

"I did not kill him," the valet growled in frustration. "It was simple enough to pull the chain out on the pretext of helping him change his shirt before bedtime. He was too foxed to notice the chain was missing, and early next morning, I snuck back into the room and replaced it."

She twirled the cigarette between her gloved fingers. "You gave me the jewels that afternoon. Father was alive then."

He grabbed her shoulders, his eyes blazing, "Exactly. Why would I need to go back and murder him after I had been successful?"

"You will not be suspected," Elizabeth soothed him. "You couldn't be."

The valet glanced away.

She continued with a touch of bitterness. "You have Mother wrapped around your little finger. She wouldn't let anything happen to you."

"Lizzy, I admit she has tried to seduce me, but I swear I have remained faithful to you. I love you and only you, the light of my love, the other half of my soul, well-bred mother of my future children—"

"I know, noggin dear. I believe you. I just wish this scheme of yours had worked. We would have been married by now."

"We can still marry. Run away with me right this moment, Lizzy. No more of this game. We have the finances now. We can go to Scotland. I have a man willing to buy the jewels staying in the village. We can sell it to him and buy a house, some sheep—"

"We can't," Elizabeth whispered unhappily.

"Why the devil not? Your father's funeral is over, nothing is stopping you now."

"We cannot because we have no money, Richard. How will we live?"

"The jewels are worth a lot more than you think—"

"The jewels are stolen," Elizabeth said shortly.

The valet's mouth dropped open. He said slowly, "Are you feeling all right? I know the jewels are stolen. We stole them."

"No, I mean you stole them and gave them to me. I kept them in a secret drawer in my desk, and now they are gone."

"Are you saying that I spent six months pretending to be a darned valet, plotted to steal the jewels, stole them, thereafter worried about being found out and suffered nightmares . . . Now those very jewels have been stolen again."

"Yes, yes and yes," she said, her shoulders sagging in defeat. "Someone stole them from me."

"It has to be that bloody rotten governess," he burst out.

"Perhaps," Elizabeth bit her lip.

"Perhaps? Is that all you can say? You were responsible for hiding the jewels, and after all, I went through, you should have thought of a safer place to keep them, you fool! I don't care how you do it, Miss Elizabeth Sedley, but I want you to get the jewels back, or I am going to tell your family your entire plan. I will admit it all to Adair. How I am an impoverished earl here by your request, your entire plot to hoodwink your own family . . . and I am not going to marry you either. You will have nowhere to go, no family, no husband—"

"Are the jewels worth more to you than I am?"

"I have seen you making eyes at Adair, trying to trap him into marriage. If he shows you so much as a hint of interest, you will forget all about me."

"What are you trying to say?"

"Find the jewels," he said in a dark, dangerous voice.

Elizabeth watched him forcefully stub the cigarette out and leave. Her face was pale, and her eyes wide and hurt.

Lucy couldn't help but feel sorry for the girl.

Chapter 27

After Elizabeth had left, Lucy turned to Lord Adair. "The theft and murder are not related."

He stood up and brushed off his breeches.

"You knew," she accused, noticing the lack of surprise on his face.

"I knew it was a possibility," he conceded.

"Now, what do I do?" she moaned. "I am being blamed for two thefts and a murder."

"Would you like my help?"

"I don't trust anyone."

Lord Adair shrugged and moved towards the door.

After a moment, Lucy ran after him, "You are supposed to convince me to trust you. You are meant to play the hero and tell me that you cannot abandon a damsel in distress no matter how much I object."

"Was I supposed to say that?"

"Yes and that it is against your honour to leave a lady dangling in danger."

"Instead, shall I say that I respect your wishes? I am certain you are capable of getting out of this pickle on your own. I am learning to have faith in you."

Lucy scowled. "I wish you would have a little less faith in me."

"Did you say something?"

"Nothing whatsoever."

They cautiously peeked out of the door. Spooner was nowhere to be seen.

"Shall we?" he asked, offering her an arm and gesturing towards the house.

Lucy dug her nails into his elbow and smiled up sweetly. "Yes, let's go back, my lord."

They walked for a few minutes in silence.

The sun was bright, but a cold breeze soon started up. The wind grew stronger, whipping the scarf off Lucy's head.

She shivered and pulled the scarf back up to cover her ears. He helped her tie it more securely under her chin.

She smiled her thanks and observed, "Some people are funny."

"Very funny," he agreed and resumed walking.

"I mean odd funny," she corrected, racing up behind him and once again gripping his arm. "I thought I knew the valet."

"Clearly, you didn't."

She continued placidly, "You would think you know everything about a person and then next moment splat."

"Splat?"

"Yes, splat. The truth slaps you in the face like a dish of half-baked pie."

"Fruit pie," he agreed. "Sticky."

She nodded and looked far off into the distance. "There was a girl once at the Brooding Cranesbill. Hannah. She was a small, grubby little thing. I often found her weeping in the broom closet. She would cower whenever I tried to speak to her. One day I convinced her to confide in me. I truly wanted to know what was troubling the poor little thing."

"I truly don't," he remarked.

She ignored him and continued. "She told me how she had found a little hare in the grounds behind the orphanage. She had started feeding it, playing with it, made a pet of it. The older girls . . . they roasted the hare and ate it."

"Tragic."

"They did the same to the little chick Hannah had found abandoned in a nest. Twisted its neck. My heart bled. I appealed to Miss Summer to punish such dreadful cruel creatures."

"And the culprits were boiled and hung out to dry. A very happy ending. Well done."

"Nothing of the sort. Miss Summer discovered the culprit, my lord. She found out that a hare had truly been roasted and eaten, a chick with a twisted neck had been found, but she also found out that none of the older girls was to blame."

He sighed and patted her hand, sympathetically, "No, it was Hannah herself who did it, was it not?"

"Yes," she brooded. "Such a convincing liar and so young ... I wonder what makes them so?"

He didn't reply but quickened his pace. She had to hasten her steps to keep up.

A chill crept up under her skirts and started sneaking its way upwards.

"It's getting colder," she grumbled after a few moments.

"Your senses are in excellent working order. Shall I applaud?"

"You are cold too," she said, noting his testy tone. "Or hungry," she added as an afterthought.

"I would appreciate a few minutes of silence."

"You want me to stop talking?"

"Not all. I was requesting the trees and the bushes to give me a few minutes of peace and quiet. I find they rustle a lot."

"You don't have to be sarcastic—" She stopped abruptly, her eyes pinned to the ground a few feet in front of her.

"Miss Trotter?" He tugged her hand on his arm.

"A moment," she gasped. "I think I found it."

"Found what?"

"The jewels," she replied in a hushed voice.

He looked around. "Where?"

"There," she pointed through excited lips.

On the ground, before her, the bright sun cascaded down on a few pieces of perfectly round dark stones. The clean, white snow seemed to be cradling them, making them shine even brighter.

Her heart starting beating so loudly that she could hear it.

He made a warning sound.

She ignored him and slowly started walking forward as if afraid the entire thing was an illusion, and any moment it would burst like a soap bubble and disintegrate.

"Miss Trotter—"

"Hush," she waved him off and crouched on the ground.

Her eyes sparkled. Had she come upon the jewels? She bent lower.

"What are you doing, Miss Trotter?"

"Don't they look like jewels?" she asked.

Her gloved fingers reached out towards them . . . almost touching . . . an inch more and . . .

"They are rabbit droppings, my dear."

Her hand slowly retreated.

She giggled.

His lips quirked. "I didn't think you would have been able to smile, Miss Trotter. Not after the conversation we overheard between Elizabeth and the Valet."

"I have something to smile about."

"What's that?"

"The large moody bird didn't peck us to death."

Lord Adair chuckled reluctantly. "There is that."

"Besides, what's the point of living if you don't like it?"

He eyed her thoughtfully.

She tilted her face up to the sun letting the rays soak into her cold thirsty skin, "Besides, tears do not help. They cloud your vision."

He smiled. "You are admirable, Miss Trotter."

"Admirable enough to be employed?" she asked him cheekily.

He just shook his head in amusement and prudently remained silent for the rest of the walk back to Rudhall.

Chapter 28

Miss Summer had often said that if you lose a toe, then be thankful that you still have a leg, or if you get burnt porridge for dinner, then be grateful for the water to wash it all down.

Lucy wondered what she should be thankful for in her present predicament. Should she be pleased that she was not yet dead, or may not be dead shortly, or that at least she had lived her life as a human being and not a fruit fly?

She tucked the blanket under her restless feet. It would be a while before she became warm enough to fall asleep. She used the time to analyse all that she had discovered.

Theft and murder were not related. The valet stole the jewels and gave them to Elizabeth, and thereafter someone stole those jewels from Elizabeth.

A tiny frown creased her forehead. Who would go looking for the jewels in Elizabeth's room? Was it one of the servants who discovered it by accident? But not a single servant had disappeared from the manor. Granted, the scullery maid was a bit dim, but even she would have enough sense to run like the devil if she had stolen so much as a spoon.

She turned over and buried her cold nose in the warm pillow.

"What are you thinking?" Aunt Sedley asked. She was lying next to Lucy. Her eyes were closed, and her head hovered over a frightened pillow.

"Will you move farther away? The cold is wafting towards me," Lucy complained, through chattering teeth.

"It is not my fault that I lost all the warmth when I died," Aunt Sedley replied sulkily.

Lucy gritted her teeth and refrained from comment. She didn't want the spirit to complain once again of her insensitivity. Besides, Aunt Sedley had helped her deal with Ian.

Aunt Sedley's transparent lashes lifted, and she turned over to face Lucy. "Is something troubling you, my dear?"

"Who could have stolen the jewels from Elizabeth and why? It doesn't make sense," Lucy replied.

"Three people could have done it."

"Three?"

Aunt Sedley nodded sagely. "Firstly, it is clear the valet is not loyal to Elizabeth. He came here to steal the jewels."

"True."

"What if the valet gave Elizabeth the jewels and then stole them back? He could have done it to keep the jewels and break off an unwanted engagement."

Lucy sat up and hugged her knees. "And the second person," she said brightening, "could be Elizabeth herself. She could have found out about the valet's infidelity. She is no fool. She must have realised that he was spending almost all his nights with her mother, which is why—"

"She pretended the jewels were stolen from her. For sweet, sweet revenge," Aunt Sedley finished rubbing her hands together.

"And lastly," Lucy mused with a shiver, "it could be the murderer who knew the theft, and the killing was not related. Hence, he or she went looking for the jewels and found them in Elizabeth's drawer."

Aunt Sedley sighed. "So we are back where we began."

Lucy moaned and fell back on the pillow. This time she brought her feet up and caught her frozen toes in her warm hands.

Her head was starting to hurt. Time was running out, the family was getting impatient. She was the one person who was expendable. No one would feel too bad if she was tossed into the sacrificial fire.

She would have to speed things up. Throw caution to the wind and start searching more aggressively. She decided to become a hound and place her nose close to the ground and sniff with all her might until she caught the right scent.

Aunt Sedley snored loudly beside her head.

Lucy burrowed her head under the pillow and closed her eyes. What she needed was a good night's sleep. She had a long day ahead . . . but thinking and doing were two different things.

Her eyes refused to close, her limbs refused to relax, and plans hopped, skipped and rolled enthusiastically in her mind.

She slept not a wink, and before she knew it, the sun had crawled up the horizon.

***

The next morning while the servants were having breakfast, Lucy went sniffing in the valet's room.

It was a neat room, bigger than her own and dust-free. The clothes were beautifully folded and arranged in the cupboard, the shoes neatly lined up at the bottom like an army of disciplined soldiers.

Lucy pulled up her sleeves and settled them well above her elbows.

She was now an experienced rummager and an explorer. If she had been given a chance at this point, she was certain she would have found a way to cut the spice route in half.

She felt so deft, so skilled, and so proficient in all this spy business that she was sure a hop would have taken her to Africa, a skip to India and a double twist and a short jump straight to the Americas.

At this point, nothing could be hidden from her keen eye and sharp wolf-like hearing. Her expert eyeballs swept around the tidy room and landed on the bed. The white sheet was pulled taut enough to frighten away wrinkles.

Her suspicious eyebrows rose, and she pounced on the plump pillows. She discovered a glittering gold watch hidden between tufts of feathers.

Pocketing the watch, she raised her nose and sniffed again. The room smelled like oiled flowers.

She soon found the source of the putrid stench. A green bottle of 'Elusive lotion for warty buttocks made from the freshest French blooms' was emanating powerful fumes from a drawer of the small wooden side table.

She hurriedly replaced the glass bottle and continued her search. It wasn't long before she discovered the loose board under the bed. She prised it open, breaking a fingernail in the process, and found love letters from lots of different women, a silver brooch, a set of fine clothes and a pair of expensive leather shoes.

The explorer in her sighed dejectedly while pocketing the silver brooch.

She crawled out in disappointment. It had taken her almost an hour to search the room, and by the end of it, she was certain the jewels were not here.

She slowly walked down the corridor towards her room. Her head was bent low, and her eyes were glazed over in deep thought.

"Oof," she exclaimed as someone ran into her.

The valet brushed past without apologising.

She narrowed her eyes. The back of his neck was scarlet.

Her gaze sharpened as she looked up and down the hallway. Why had the valet been in this part of the house? The only room down that end was hers—

Her eyes widened, and she sprinted across the corridor and flung open her room door.

At first glance, everything seemed to be in place, but she soon discovered a crumpled petticoat pushed right at the back of her cupboard.

Her brows furrowed thoughtfully. She recalled folding the petticoat and placing it on the top shelf of the cupboard. It had a long tear in it. She had meant to mend it ... She looked down at the bright yellow scrunched up cloth and shook her head in amusement.

While she had been searching through the valet's room for the jewels, he had been searching hers.

She closed the cupboard and leaned back against it. So, if the valet hadn't stolen the jewels from Elizabeth, then who the devil had?

She closed her eyes and took a deep breath and let it out slowly.

The theft and the murder were not related, and stealing did not take half as much courage or brains as murdering someone did. Which meant that any halfwit could have pinched the jewels. A fat headed simpleton could have easily crept into Elizabeth's room and—

Her eyes flew open.

"I'll be bound," she said softly, "that blithering idiot, no good oozing scab, Ian Percival Humphrey Sedley, must have stolen the blasted jewels."

***

Lucy entered Ian's room an hour before dinner time. She had carefully chosen that hour for her investigation, knowing that Ian would have started on his daily consumption of whiskey and it would be a good few hours before he became tippled enough to roll back into the room to sleep.

Unfortunately, Lucy had failed to take into consideration the fact that a man like Ian could fall in love.

You see, Ian had been slapped in his empty head that morning by a vision of a charmingly plump, auburn-haired girl with lush pink cheeks. He knew neither her name nor what she did, but what he did know was that his empty head was now filled with songs and dances, poetry and paintings, stars and moonbeams.

Lucy learned all about this beautiful creature while trembling behind the thick, emerald green curtains. She had concealed herself as soon as she had heard Ian come strolling down the hallway, whistling a merry tune.

Ian was drunk on love. He had no need for whiskey and brandy. He said as much to the rose carpet. He also told the cupboards how fine the curls were atop the round head that he had decided to marry.

He informed the comb, as he carefully parted his oiled hair, that he imagined his beloved's feet were small and delicate. But even if, he clarified to the judgemental sofa, the feet turned out to be big, fat lumps, he would still adore them.

When he fell silent, and the silence continued to stretch, Lucy dared to peek out from behind the curtain.

She found Ian lying on the bed, spinning a yellow flower in one hand while the other arm rested under his head. He was staring at the roof loopily; his mouth was open and drool glimmered on his cheek in the firelight. He appeared to be daydreaming.

"Ian," Lady Sedley charged in.

Lucy ducked her head back behind the drapes and resumed trembling.

"Mother," Ian said.

Lucy heard his feet hit the floor as he sprang up into a sitting position.

"Are you feeling all right, my sweet little boy?"

Lucy's eyebrows shot up.

"Yes, I am. And I have told you before not to talk to me like that," he complained.

"You weren't getting oiled in the library. I was worried, sweetums."

"Mother," he whined, though not convincingly enough.

"Oh, look, your hair is wet," Lady Sedley continued. "You will catch your death. Do you want me to dry your hair, ickle baby?"

"Aww, no, Ma. I am not a baby," he said, a hint of enjoyment lacing his voice.

"No one is here. Can't I spoil my favourite little boo-boo?"

Lucy closed her eyes. She felt like laughing and crying at the same time. Who would have thought the big bad Ian became a small little boy in private around his mother.

"Mother, don't rub my head so hard," Ian complained. "The cloth is rough."

"Hush now," Lady Sedley murmured lovingly, "my delicate child."

"I am not delicate. I am a man, and you will miss your dinner," Ian said. This time he sounded impatient.

"Are you truly feeling fine?" Lady Sedley asked again. "Well, then come along now for dinner."

"No," he replied sulkily.

"I asked the cook to make some sweet bread," Lady Sedley coaxed.

"With raisins?" he asked, cheering up.

"Plenty of them," she replied.

Lucy breathed a sigh of relief when mother and son departed for dinner.

After that, she did what she had become used to doing. She quickly and efficiently searched the room.

She found plenty of empty bottles, snuff boxes and fine clothes, but no jewels. Biting her lip, she replaced everything and departed.

Peter's room was next on her list. And his was the only room in the house she had yet to search. If the jewels were not there either . . ..

Chapter 29

Lucy crouched low and peeked inside the bedroom.

Peter was trying to warm a porcupine in bed.

Lucy cursed under her breath. Was no one ready to leave their rooms on time tonight?

"Are you warm, little one?" Peter asked the porcupine whom he had covered with a blanket and placed in the middle of the bed.

A little nose poked out from underneath the dark wool and quivered.

"I suppose I will have to keep you in my room until you feel better," he said, gently tapping the nose. "I don't want to leave you alone, but the kittens have to be fed."

He placed a bit of bark next to the porcupine's nose and stood up.

Lucy quickly scuttled away from the door and hid behind a large potted plant. She waited until the sound of Peter's footsteps faded away before darting into his room.

The porcupine tucked its nose back under the blanket at her entrance.

Peter's room was near the staircase. Hence, every few moments, Lucy froze in terror when someone went up or down the stairs. When she was not frozen, she searched the room.

She found lots of cotton wool, heaps of old clothes, blankets and glass jars filled with strange liquids and powders.

"Come down, you rascal," Lady Sedley yelled.

Lucy squished the funny smelling leaves she had been inspecting in fright.

"Don't you dare make those cheeky faces at me," Lady Sedley continued.

Cheeky faces? Lucy frowned and tiptoed towards the door.

"Peter, come and take your baboon away. The blasted creature has leapt over the gate again. I am certain he is going to my room to steal the sugared pineapples. Come here, you monster. How dare you show me your scarlet bottom? You will be cooked; I tell you."

The bell tinkled as the wooden gate swung open.

Lucy did not wait for Lady Sedley to ascend and begin chasing Palmer around the house. She threw the leaves on the carpet, sprang out the door and pelted down the hallway, all before Lady Sedley had taken three steps.

Back in her room, she scrubbed her hands with water, trying to get rid of the odd scent of leaves. She rubbed her hands' raw busy thinking about what she had not found in Peter's room.

The jewels.

The blasted elusive cursed pieces of stones were not in anyone's room. Not the servants, not the family . . . She threw the soaking muslin cloth at the wall in frustration.

Things were looking horribly grim.

***

The kitchen fell silent the moment Lucy entered.

She ignored the silence and filled a cup with steaming coffee.

After a tense moment, the butler resumed conversation with the valet. "It came to my ears late last night that Lady Sedley has demanded that the killer be discovered within the next two days. The stress of living with a murderer," Here the butler slanted a look at Lucy, "is bothering her nerves. She said that if the murderer is not caught and the jewels retrieved, then she will be forced to ask Lord Adair to leave. She has already written to the Duke of Henley who lives a few miles south to come and finish off the investigations."

"She couldn't ask Lord Adair to leave, could she? She wouldn't dare," the cook gasped.

"She won't demand it, I suppose, but she will request him to speed up the investigations," the butler mused. "And when the Duke of Henley arrives, he can have a go at convincing Lord Adair."

"But the Duke of Henley knows nothing about the murder," the valet objected.

"Lady Sedley has apprised him of the facts. She wrote to him about her suspicions, and he is bound to agree with them," the butler replied.

The valet leaned back in his chair, while his hand spun a shiny copper coin on the table. "In other words, the duke is coming in two days . . . to sentence Miss Trotter."

The cup slipped through Lucy's fingers and crashed to the ground.

No one moved to clean up the mess.

The butler shrugged and spoke after a long silence. "It's time to take the tray up for Mr Sedley. He plans to go riding after an early breakfast this morning."

***

Lucy slowly walked down the stairs towards her room. A piece of stale cake trembled in her hand as the valet's words swam in her head.

She had two days. Two short days of freedom.

She paused on the steps wondering if she should once again hunt through the valet's things. Perhaps she had missed something. She had a strong feeling that Lady Sedley and the valet had killed Lord Sedley together.

After all, Lady Sedley had never looked this blooming happy when the old man had been alive. Her children would no longer suffer, the small treasures in the house could be sold, and the house let. A substantial fortune—

Palmer snatched the cake out of her hand, pulling her back to the present. The pugs at her feet licked the dropped crumbs.

She didn't mind. Her appetite had fled a good while ago.

It was no good. She had searched the valet's room well enough. She was grasping at straws, trying to find something to occupy her mind and keep the panic at bay.

All her plans were now exhausted. Not a single bright idea flickered in her mind, and a hint of hopelessness started worming its way into her heart.

She entered her room and found Spinoza perched upon the cupboard.

Spinoza flapped his dark wings and cocked his head as if inspecting Lucy's miserable face. He squawked once and flew away as if wanting nothing to do with unhappy creatures.

That was it.

She had been given the cut by a darned raven. She could no longer pretend that the world was full of roses, the air scented with lilies and the manor full of pleasant-faced, cheerful humans beings.

No. The manor was lousy.

The animals didn't love her.

The servants hated her.

The family loathed her.

The orphanage didn't want her.

She had been accused of crimes she had never committed.

A spirit was haunting her.

No one loved her.

She was a miserable, pathetic, wretched thing, and she could no longer take it anymore.

The river bubbled over and burst its banks. She opened her mouth and let out a heart-wrenching wail.

She sobbed and howled banging her head on the pillow.

Tears cascaded down her face enough to fill a bucket—not one of those small buckets but a large one. Large enough to contain an entire family's weeks' worth of soiled clothes—Her heart felt like it was melting from sadness, and her soul seemed to cry and shake at the unfairness of it all.

Lord Adair's head appeared at the door.

Lucy banged her head once more on the pillow before unhappily eyeing him through a curtain of thick brown hair.

He appeared to be pleased and relieved at finding her thus. "Carry on," he said, gesturing at the pillow and popped his head back out.

"Wait," Lucy yelled, wiping her nose on the back of her sleeve and throwing the pillow aside.

It was time to face her biggest fear and take risks. Only one man could save her now, and she had to take the plunge and put all her trust in him.

She had to talk to Lord William Hartell Adair and if needed, lie prostrate on the ground before him, grab his feet and refuse to let go until he agreed to help her.

Chapter 30

"I am skimming over deep waters heading for the waterfall," Lucy said the moment she spotted Lord Adair in the library. "I am about to tip over the edge and crash into the swirling abyss below," she continued.

He dipped the quill in ink and spoke without looking up. "Come to the point, Miss Trotter."

"Right, then. I am a harmless little beetle about to be squished by a giant boot, and it is at times like this when one has to take a risk."

"I see," he replied, signing off the letter he had been writing.

"I feel like I have eaten too many cakes, and now I am stuck between two slabs of stone."

Lord Adair put the sealed envelope away and squeezed the bridge of his nose.

Lucy stepped closer to him. "I am left with no choice. I have hunted, I have stolen, I have chased and been chased, and yet here I am."

"Yes?"

"Swinging like a church bell between life and death."

"Do you need my help?"

Lucy's shoulders dropped. "Something of the sort."

"You concede defeat and admit that I am going to solve the crime faster than you are?"

"Now look here," Lucy snapped, pulling out a chair and plonking herself down on it. "I didn't say I am stopping my investigations. In fact, I have come to share all I know. You can be gallant. After all, you are a renowned thief catcher. You have a lot of experience, but I may know something you don't. We can air out our suspicions and discuss our progress. You can help me, I can help you—"

"I thought you did not need my help."

"Things have changed."

"I see you have found out about Lady Sedley's threat, and now it's either accept my help or hang."

Lucy pressed her lips together.

Lord Adair softened his tone. "Tell me, who do you suspect?"

Lucy eyed him suspiciously. After a moment's hesitation, she told him about all her discoveries.

He listened quietly, nodding encouragement every now and then.

She finally relaxed back in her seat and said. "It has to be Lady Sedley and the valet."

"Lady Sedley was with Peter at the time of the murder," Lord Adair replied. "And the valet was with the butler in the kitchen."

"Peter could have lied to protect his mother."

"He could have, but then you have overheard two conversations between Lady Sedley and Peter, and in both those instances Lady Sedley seemed to be certain that neither he nor she left the morning room."

"Ian?" Lucy suggested next.

Lord Adair frowned. "He is in debt, and if he does not get the money, then he may have to go to prison again."

She leaned forward eagerly. "He has the biggest reason to kill his father—"

"But . . . "

"But?"

"He did not commit the crime."

"How can you be so certain?"

He replied thoughtfully, "Ian has a short temper, but he is also a coward and incredibly foolish. He couldn't have killed anyone, let alone do it so neatly."

"That is mere speculation. He could have a lot going on behind that sap skull. You never know what is in another person's mind."

He nodded appreciatively. "I agree, which was why I confirmed with Ian's debtor that on the day of the murder Ian had been with him until six in the evening. When Ian did go home, he found Lady Sedley ranting about the missing jewels. She was in no state to be coherent and failed to tell him about his father's death. Ian had been counting on the jewels to pay his debt, and he stormed out of the house in anger. He arrived at the village and met me at the inn and told me all about the theft. The doctor informed us both of Lord Sedley's death and the shock on his face on hearing the news had been genuine."

"The servants?"

"All accounted for."

"Elizabeth?"

"Was in the nursery with the children."

Lucy nodded. However evil she wanted to believe Elizabeth was, the girl did love the children. She rocked her chair back and forth thoughtfully. "You do not suspect the servants or the family members. The only person left is . . . " She lifted her lashes in fright. "You think I killed him."

Lord Adair chose to keep silent this time.

"And you think I stole the jewels as well."

"From the way things are going, it appears so."

She paled. "I know I am innocent, and according to you, so is everyone else. Then who killed him, Lord Adair? Aunt Sedley's ghost?"

He smiled. "Something of the sort."

"Well, I can assure you it wasn't her."

"Her?"

"Aunt Sedley. She told me so herself."

"She did?"

"Why, yes, she floated into my room the other day and told me all about it. She thought it highly unfair of the family to blame her. She can't even touch a human being, let alone harm them. She can frighten the wits out of you, though, but Lord Sedley was clearly stabbed—"

"Miss Trotter," he interrupted, "I think you have been out in the sun too long."

"The sun rarely shines at this time of the year, my lord."

"Well, then the pressure of being accused of murder has been too much for your delicate mind. I am afraid you are teetering on edge—"

"Eh?"

"I don't know how to say this," he said with a concerned and kindly look in his eyes, "but you may be partially mad or totally imbecile. It is hard to say—"

"I am sane as you are, my lord," she said stiffly.

"You should sleep for a few hours. It will do you good. Have a hot cup of soothing tea, a warming pan at your feet, and you shall feel wonderful—"

"My lord, are you going to help me or not?"

"I am trying to help you."

"Help me find the killer."

"Leave it to me."

"How can I leave it to you? I am the one who stands accused," she exclaimed.

"Everyone leaves it to me, Miss Trotter. No one has dared to interfere before now. They have faith in my capabilities."

"Well, I don't."

He shrugged and pulled a fresh sheet of paper towards himself and began writing.

She watched him for a few moments. When he didn't look up, she said bitterly, "You have spent the entire time finding alibis for everyone in the house. How can I trust you?"

He ignored her.

She shook her head in disbelief. She had assumed the man was a rational, intelligent creature and someone she had hoped deep in her heart was her ally . . . someone who wanted to find out the truth.

Now, it seemed, she truly was alone.

She sprang out of the chair and placed her trembling palms on the edge of the table. "If you believe I did it, then why not arrest me and be done with it?"

He looked up then. "I never said you did it, Miss Trotter, though I have a hunch on who it could be. Be patient, I am waiting for proof. The murderer is clever and has left behind no clues."

"What am I supposed to do until then? I cannot sit idle."

"You should."

She scowled. "And what will your next step be?"

"Lurk in the dark. When you know who the culprit is, then it is only a matter of time before he or she makes a mistake. I am waiting for that mistake, Miss Trotter."

Chapter 31

Thunder roared ominously. The clouds rushed forward and gobbled up the sun. Lightning streaked across the sky, and hail rattled the windows of Rudhall Manor.

"I know," Lucy growled at the great being that controlled all destinies, "that I am in mortal peril. You don't need to make the sky roar for me to understand. My head is not stuffed with cotton wool."

The great being who controlled all destinies seemed to mockingly raise his bushy eyebrows, for the wind picked up speed and the hail clattered harder on the panes.

Lucy narrowed her eyes, clasped her hands behind her back and resumed pacing the hallway.

The conversation with Lord Adair had been futile. He had neither calmed her fears nor left her a trembling mess. What he had done was to make her realise that all her findings were worth nought.

She once again suspected everyone and believed no one.

She absently chewed on a ragged nail. At the Brooding Cranesbill, Miss Hardy had been partial to a few girls, and because of her fragmented vision, she had often ended up unjustly punishing some innocent orphans.

What if she too was looking at the problem through a pinhole? Perhaps if she scratched away at the hole and made it bigger, she would come upon the truth.

She recalled looking at a painting a five-year-old girl had drawn once. She had oohed and aahed at the blob thinking the young girl had sketched out a stem of a mushroom.

The girl had informed her that it was, in fact, an elephant leg. Elephants, the girl had importantly continued, were large animals. So large that she couldn't possibly draw the entire animal on such a small sheet of paper. After that, Lucy's praise for the painting had been genuine. It was a novel way of thinking.

Was she once again looking at the mushroom stem and not the elephant?

She tried to expand her mind. She pretended she was floating along with Aunt Sedley a few feet away from Rudhall Manor and inspected the deformed architecture from afar.

It was a crooked, grey manor that rose up from the ground like a lopsided warty toad squatting on a gently sloping hill.

The numerous windows gleaming together in a straight line on the lower half of the building made it seem as if the toad was grinning like a lecherous landlord.

The windows glinted harder in the sunlight, flashing yellow like chipped, stained teeth as if daring her to come closer.

She bravely propelled her imaginary self-nearer to the building and found herself peering in through a glassless window.

An empty room lay beyond, devoid of human life, neglected and rotting away.

She moved from window to window, flying around the building taking note of the dozens of rooms that lay empty and unused visited only by rats and spiders.

She blinked back to the present with a crucial question blazing in her mind.

Was someone hiding in one of the locked rooms in the house?

Even the grounds were extensive, sprawling and overgrown, she mused, as she recalled the abandoned orangery she and Lord Adair had hidden themselves in to evade the Egyptian crane.

Anyone could be living in such a building. It was ideal for someone seeking peace, solitude or a hideout.

She frowned. But why would anyone choose to dwell with spiders and rats? Was it a poor vagrant or someone more sinister?

Lord Sedley had been despised by his own family members and servants. It was possible that there were still others who loathed him. He could have wronged a friend, cheated an acquaintance or insulted a sensitive relative.

Was that what Lord Adair was hinting at? Did one of the rooms hide an old angry relative who had crawled out at five in the evening that fateful day?

Lucy skidded to a halt.

It was all too possible. A shoeless woman with long matted hair could have slithered out of one of the abandoned rooms.

Hungry for tea she would have meandered down the hallway when all of a sudden she would have paused and cocked her skeletal head . . . She had heard something . . . a snore . . . a dark, treacherous snore emerging from Lord Sedley's ill-omened nostril.

She would have smiled, her front tooth would have twinkled, and a dagger would have appeared in her hand—a long silver dagger with a sharp edge that glittered along with her twinkling tooth.

The dagger had shimmered, the tooth had twinkled.

The tooth had twinkled, and the dagger had shimmered.

Dagger, tooth . . . dagger, tooth . . . tooth, dagger . . . tooth, dagger and—

Stab, stab, stab, slash.

Lord Sedley was dead.

After the horrible deed, she would have wiped the knife clean on her moth-eaten, filthy dress, stolen a piece of cake, two spice biscuits and a cigar lying on the study table and slithered back to her room.

Lighting the cigar, she had puffed away enjoying the peace that the act of murdering a nincompoop had brought to her soul.

She had puffed and puffed and puffed while the smoke from her cigar had formed visions in the air. They reminded her of the happy days when she had been Lord Sedley's mistress.

The smoke had curled and reformed to throw up darker memories that spoke of neglect and abandonment.

The grey mist had then swirled faster and faster, becoming dangerous like a gathering storm as she recalled how she had threatened to tell his wife of their affair.

Lord Sedley, with all his faults, had loved his wife. He had locked away his mistress in one of the many empty rooms of the manor to prevent the truth from coming out. He had kept her like a bird in a golden cage until one fateful day she found a way to escape her room—

Lucy ran into a standing armour, and her fantastic tale came to an abrupt end. She rubbed her bruised head, waiting for the stars floating in front of her eyes to disappear entirely before making way towards her bedroom.

This new line of thought where someone hiding in the manor had murdered Lord Sedley seemed to ring right. She pondered over this new discovery for a while. She dissected the thought, upturned it, peered at it from side to side, bottom to top and then back again.

Her face was flushed and her brow fevered by the time she had finished thinking. The sweat on her skin seemed to mock the flecks of snow that had replaced the noisy rain outside.

She entered her room and walked up to the basin filled with icy water. She quickly splashed her face and wiped her face dry with a muslin cloth before the muscles in her face could freeze.

Refreshed, she once again began plucking at the thought that a stranger was residing in Rudhall Manor. A stranger filled with bitterness and hate who skulked around in the dark and went about stabbing people.

And while she plucked away at the thought, teased it and unravelled it, her eyes landed on a beautifully carved wooden box sitting in the middle of the bed.

It was a medium-sized rosewood box, hard to miss against the white bed sheet. The top of the box was painted in muted greens and soft pinks, while the catch was polished gold.

She gulped.

A pretty box, a box that looked expensive—a box that was not hers—was sitting in the middle of the bed.

She looked around the room and swayed. Her green travelling dress was draped on the back of the chair. Her grey slippers sat neatly in one corner. The half-finished letter to her bosom friend Charlotte had ended up on the floor.

It was definitely her room, but—her eyes swivelled back to the bed—the box . . . the box was not hers.

With trembling legs, she moved closer to the box. It was as if she was terrified; it would suddenly leap into the air and bite her.

She lurched forward and bravely touched the lid.

She was afraid of opening it and confirming her suspicions . . . .

But it had to be done.

A deep breath later, she snapped it open and stared at the contents.

Her entire body started trembling, her breath came in shallow gasps, and her eyes widened in horror.

Someone gasped behind her.

She turned around to find the butler staring at the box.

A moment later, he gave a full-throated cry which rang through the house. "I found the thief, I found the thief, I fooouuund the jewel thieeeeef!"

Lucy's knees gave away, and she collapsed on the bed. She had been looking for the jewels all over the house, and here it was, the very same jewellery box relaxing in the middle of her bed, staring up at her, looking mighty pleased with itself.

ANYA WYLDE

She was doomed.

The thick noose hopped over and began knocking insistently against her frightened head.

ANYA WYLDE

Chapter 32

What sort of a daft fool would leave a fortune on her bed, Lucy wondered. If only the butler had not come upon her at the moment of discovery, she would have shot out of Rudhall Manor, escaped to the nearest port and set sail for exotic lands.

She wondered if she would have liked living in France. She could have fashioned herself into some sort of an English countess, found a dashing lord to marry . . . or perhaps Spain. Spain was warm, and she did so love Spanish oranges. All-day she would sit on the porch eating oranges upon oranges and then some more oranges spitting out the pips trying to shoot them as far possible—

Lord Adair touched her elbow and pulled her back to the present.

"We need to tie her up," Elizabeth was saying. "I cannot have a loony murderer running around the mansion while I sleep."

Everyone had congregated in the morning room. Sixteen cups of coffee had been consumed while all shapes of eyeballs had tried to pierce Lucy's nervous skull.

"Is there no way we can send her away tonight, Lord Adair?" Lady Sedley asked. She was sitting on the sofa or rather half lying on it. Her pale hand was resting on the back of the sofa, the other draped artistically over the arm. Her thin white robe had slipped off one shoulder, and her left ankle was on shameless display.

Lord Adair ignored the ankle and the exposed white neck. "I am afraid it is late. Besides, the roads are blocked with snow. The carriage won't be able to leave the village. I don't want to take a risk in case she escapes during the journey."

Lucy widened her eyes, silently appealing to all those around her. She tried to move her facial muscles to look as innocent as possible. She begged them to take one look at her forlorn face, to dive into the depths of her pupils and splash around a bit to judge the truth for themselves. She had not stolen anything or murdered anyone.

"Her old room," Lady Sedley said stifling a yawn, "is on the first floor and has a sturdy lock." She pulled out a bunch of keys from the pocket of her robe and tossed it towards Lord Adair. "Lock her in. We can deal with her in the morning."

"Lord Sedley," Lord Adair asked, turning to Peter, "do you approve of the plan?"

Peter looked up, his expression was anguished. "You should have told me you had the jewels," he said, looking at Lucy. "I could have done something . . . anything. It wouldn't have come to this."

Elizabeth gasped. "You are feeling sorry for this creature?"

"Love has blinded you," Ian said in sympathy. "I understand all too well." He sighed heavily.

"Perhaps," Peter said softly, his eyes refusing to leave Lucy's face.

Lucy blushed and looked away. This was awful. A man was declaring his love for her for the first time in her life, and all she could wish at the moment was to silence the blithering, love-struck idiot.

Couldn't he see this was not the hour to spout such nonsense? She stood accused of crimes, and instead of saying he did not believe she could commit such acts, he was moaning about how he loved her in spite of her penchant for murder and theft.

She glared at him. He could save her instead of gently nudging her towards a high cliff and then lovingly pushing her off.

"I am going to bed," Elizabeth said. She stood up, eyed Lucy like she was a loathsome insect one final time, before gliding out of the room.

Lord Adair gripped Lucy's resigned elbow and gently steered her out of the room.

Head bent low, she allowed her elbow to be led towards her old room. A room she would have been happy to see again had the circumstances been different.

Outside the room, Lord Adair tilted her chin up and asked gently, "Do you need anything from the basement for the night? Your nightgown or a book?"

Lucy shook her head. She doubted she would be able to sleep at all.

He searched her face. When she refused to meet his gaze, he let his hand fall.

She stepped away, watching him test the keys to check which one fit the lock.

The keys jangled loudly as he sifted through, and taking advantage of the din, he said softly, "I know you are innocent."

Lucy swivelled her face towards him so fast she made herself dizzy.

"Eh?" She wasn't sure if she had heard him correctly.

The key turned in the lock, and he gestured towards the door. "This is necessary. Have patience."

"I will be dead by the time you solve this crime," Lucy whispered bitterly.

Footsteps sounded behind them.

Lord Adair pressed his lips together and slightly shook his head in warning.

She was not a halfwit, she growled to herself. She knew when to keep silent. He did not need to be so patronising. She marched into the room, her head held high.

"Do not try and do anything foolish, and do not worry," he ordered quietly just before slamming the door shut and locking her in.

Lucy worried.

If Lord Adair knew who the culprit was, then why didn't he catch the person, torture him a little bit and get him to confess the truth? Or was he trying to indulge her, telling her he knew she was innocent while he coaxed her all the way to the continent?

"I am getting married," Aunt Sedley announced whizzing into the room.

"Congratulations," Lucy said sourly.

"You can be a little more enthusiastic," Aunt Sedley grumbled. Her upside-down face danced in front of Lucy's unhappy eyeballs. "I have never been married before."

"I didn't know ghosts could marry," Lucy replied.

"Well, they can. It is in a fortnight, the wedding I mean. I wish you could attend, but only the dead are allowed to witness the ceremony. Besides, you can't fly, and I am getting married on a cloud—"

"I will attend your wedding."

"How?"

"I would be dead too. A ghost flying around. It doesn't seem so bad. I can attend your wedding. I already know a spirit . . . The noose will hurt, but after that—"

Aunt Sedley flipped in the air to stand upright. "Did something happen tonight?"

"The thief left the box of jewels on my bed. The butler caught me with it."

Aunt Sedley whistled making the pillow leap in the air, roll onto the ground and cower under the bed in fright. "Now what?"

Lucy shrugged. "We plan your wedding."

Aunt Sedley clucked sympathetically, "Make sure you wear a pretty dress when you die. You will have to wear it for the rest of eternity. We can't change clothes."

"Anything else?"

"I will find you a handsome spirit to marry. A dashing, dangerous one who will float you off your feet."

Lucy nodded.

"Miss Trotter," Aunt Sedley said gently, "you don't have to hang. You have a way out."

Lucy closed her eyes. "I know."

Aunt Sedley patted her on the head. "I have to go now. Mr Brown had something important to tell me . . . Will you be fine on your own?"

Lucy forced a smile.

"Well, then . . . I will see you later. And, Miss Trotter, don't worry. If things don't go your way . . . being a ghost is not so bad."

Lucy stayed silent.

"I will see you later," Aunt Sedley soothed one final time. "Don't forget you have a way out . . . way out . . . way out . . . ."

After the spirit's departure, Lucy pulled open the curtains and stared at the moon. It was full and bright and happy looking.

How many more moons would she get to see from earth?

The three stars standing together in a row twinkled down at her. Don't be so bloody morbid they seemed to advise her. Save your bacon they continued.

She stared at the dark frosty ground, the dew twinkling on blades of grass and the endless forest in the distance.

Aunt Sedley had been right. She had a way out, and she would have to risk it.

She had but one choice left. She would have to run away tonight.

Chapter 33

Lucy had never enjoyed snuff, but currently, she would have given anything for a sniff of the stuff. She needed something heartening. Some sort of concoction to bolster spirits, to instil courage and to put the wag in the unhappy tail.

She would have given half a leg for a bottle of brandy, even if it was the cheap stuff. But, alas, the room had been cleared out. Not a cigar, not a cigarette, not a drop of morphine lurked in any corner.

She was doomed to push on without mind-numbing solids or liquids. She had to prepare to leap into the unknown, trickle-down a makeshift rope, dash across the moonlit garden and make her way through the dark forest until she reached some far off civilisation.

She would live on birds and leaves. Drink from a stream and nibble on sweet berries. She would light a roaring fire every night using wood she had collected all day and chirrup with the birds that she had not eaten.

She would work as a maid in an inn, saving up the pennies until one day she would escape the English shores. Escape the monsters who were looking for her, who wanted to hang her for a crime she had never committed.

And then . . . and then she would stow away on a ship to India where a rajah would be befogged upon seeing her beauty and whisk her off to his palace. She would marry him and have twelve little children in twelve warm cots with twelve capable nannies.

The rosy daydream ended as she made the final knot in the bedsheet.

She had tied two curtains and a bed sheet together and added knots at various intervals to make a ladder. It was something she knew she was good at considering the number of times she had wriggled out of her room at the orphanage and hopped over the neighbour's garden to steal apples.

Next, she bound the rope around the leg of the heavy writing desk, clambered on top of the desk, threw open the window and flung the rest of the rope out of it.

She poked her head out, inspecting the ground below.

The end of her rope had disappeared into a bush.

She dashed back to the bed, shoved two pillows under her dress which she could use as a cushion, warming pan or smothering tool depending on the circumstances, knotted a shawl around her endangered neck and considered herself utterly prepared for the adventure ahead.

ANYA WYLDE

A deep breath later, she vibrated down the rope and tumbled into the bush below.

It was cold. The ground was covered in ankle-deep snow, while the full moon was gazing down at her disapprovingly.

She stuck her tongue out at the moon and started walking.

The night was bright, and she could be easily spotted. She wondered where the blasted clouds were when she wanted them.

She chose to stick close to the hedges, and crouching low darted forward hoping the shadows would conceal her.

She scuttled forward for some time flitting from one looming shadow to another, but it wasn't long before her bended knees started to complain.

Her knees demanded to be straightened. They wailed loud and high about being misused. Soon the distressed knees threatened to stiffen and play dead if things continued to go on as they were.

She had no choice. She was forced to straighten the protesting joints.

She walked upright for a while, and soon, with each new step, her fear began to diminish. And the reason for her rapidly abating fear was her internal monologue where she was trying to see the positive side of things.

Sure, a wild animal could attack her at any moment, but she was strong. Stronger than many people supposed she was. She could easily defeat the animal, lug it over her shoulders and roast it later for a late-night supper.

Or a deadly bandit could be creeping along the boundary of Rudhall Manor. She raised her chin in the air. A deadly bandit or a mangy crook couldn't frighten her. After all, she was one of them at the moment.

She would tell them about her plight, and they would sympathise . . . yes, they would sympathise with a fellow outlaw and offer her a dodgy hand and swear to protect her imperilled head.

She would become friends with these new found robbers. Join them in their mission and become the smartest, sharpest and the most infamous woman in the world.

Miss Lucy Anne Trotter, the glamorous jewel thief. It sounded right.

Her cautious steps became more confident, her fearful shuffle turned into a confident strut, and her brisk walk started warming her up as she continued to daydream.

She would wear her hair up at all times, studded with diamond pins that could unlock anything in the world. She would swirl her skirts a certain way every time she robbed someone successfully and perform an enchanting little dance. She would mingle with the likes of the regent, the king and even the world-renowned highwayman, the Falcon—

Scratch, scratch, scratch, a sound whispered through the still night.

She froze and her eyes swivelled in all directions. Her brave little heart faltered, and her brave little thoughts scampered away.

Shuk, shuk, shuk, a new sound started a moment later.

Fear in all its roaring glory slammed back into her.

Skreeeek whispered through the air.

It was close, whatever it was. Was it an animal or human, she couldn't tell.

Thump.

She jumped out of her skin and then pulled it back on. That sound had been loud enough to dispel any thought that it was her imagination.

Heart pounding, she started inching forward and soon quickened her pace. She didn't want to wait around to be discovered.

It wasn't long before she was pelting down the path.

She flew through the night, her hands flapping about her like a one-winged duck. Her feet skimmed, slipped and slid over the snow occasionally landing on a crunchy leaf or a snappy twig.

The pins in her hair abandoned ship and ran away, one of the pillows slipped out from beneath the dress and bounced towards a prickly bush, and finally, her best pair of stockings laddered from toe to hip.

All at once, her hurrying ankle slammed into something hard on the ground. She flew through the air like a baby dolphin leaping over a frothy wave and splashed onto the snow-covered ground.

Spitting the snow out of her mouth, she scrambled up into a sitting position and looked behind to see what she had tripped on.

A soft scream escaped her, and her eyes widened in horror.

A man was lying face down on the ground behind her.

Her stomach twisted sickeningly as she dared to nudge the body with her toe.

Was he dead?

A little fearfully, she pushed the man harder with her foot.

The body flipped over instead of shifting in the snow. It was lighter than she had expected.

Far lighter . . . inhumanly light.

She also realised that the body did not have a face. All she could see was white skin and no features.

Her palms turned cold, and her vision started blurring.

This was a nightmare.

A sickening sensation started blooming in her stomach, and her tongue felt dry and parched.

That horrible featureless face, white as snow, was glowing eerily in the night.

She was going to faint . . . .

A single cloud fluttering in front of the moon drifted away, and in the more vivid light, Lucy's hazy vision registered something familiar.

The body was inanimate. The skin was not skin but plain white cloth. It was a large doll in the shape of a man.

Chapter 34

Lucy giggled hysterically. Who would make a doll that size? Did the children make it for some silly game?

The doll even had clothes on. Late Lord Sedley's clothes.

The laughter died in her tonsils.

She frowned and reached out to touch the gilt buttons when a hiss to her right arrested her fingers in mid-air.

Dark, feral eyes shimmered in the moonlight.

Palmer, the baboon, sat watching her every move, a knife glinting in his small hairy hands.

She gulped.

Something was dreadfully wrong. The very air encompassing Palmer seemed to throb with danger.

She looked back at the doll.

The bright moon illuminated dark criss-cross lines on the doll's chest.

Her heart filled with dread. The lines were slashes made by a dagger.

Her eyes widened in understanding as the broken puzzle floated together and formed a whole, vivid and dangerous picture.

A myriad of scenes raced by in her mind.

Everyone had an alibi in the house.

Lord Adair's words that it was something like a ghost.

Lady Sedley screaming at the baboon for having leapt over the gate to steal the sugared pineapples.

The images came in quick succession now . . . Palmer eating with a spoon, picking nits out of Ian's hair, faithfully copying several of Peter's gestures . . .

Using a dagger to stab Lord Sedley six times in the chest.

Palmer moved, wrenching her back to the present. His large, dark body slowly came to rest on his hands.

She stumbled backwards in fright, and her foot landed on something sharp that dug through her thin boots. Stifling a scream, she looked down and found a spade jutting out from underneath her boot.

Holding back the growing panic, she cast a desperate eye around herself, searching for a means of escape and spotted a freshly dug ditch nearby.

Her eyes flickered from the neat length of the ditch to the large dummy.

Her heart thundered in her ribs, and she lurched backwards in horror.

It wasn't a ditch at all but a grave for the doll.

ANYA WYLDE

"It is a pity you discovered us," Peter's voice said in her ear.

Something cold and hard jabbed her spine.

She stopped breathing.

"Stand up," he ordered.

"You are very clever," she said, her voice thick with fear.

He slipped an arm around her waist and pulled her up. "We are going to walk towards the animal house now. Don't try and scream."

"You trained Palmer. He leapt over the gate, entered the room and stabbed Lord Sedley in the chest when he was asleep."

"Lower your tone," he whispered, his fingers digging into her waist in a warning.

She allowed herself to be led in silence for a bit. Her brain was working harder and clearer than ever before. Every sound, every colour suddenly seemed enhanced in her mind's eye.

"What are you going to do with me?" she asked.

"Kill you."

She swallowed nervously. "You won't get away with another murder."

"But you won't be murdered, Miss Trotter. You will leave a note stating how you couldn't bear the guilt of having blood on your hands before I shoot you. According to the world, you would have committed suicide."

Terror seized her limbs.

Peter had to begin dragging her through the snow for her feet were now refusing to move.

"The animals will miss me," she said, trying to appeal to his softer side.

Peter stopped walking. "True. You are a good person, Miss Trotter, and I don't have anything against you. I don't want to harm you, but I am left with no other choice."

A shadow moved in the corner of her eye.

"You planted the jewels in my room," she said, desperate to keep him talking. Someone was nearby listening to every word they were saying, "so that I became a definite suspect. I was always meant to be sacrificed."

"Curious," he replied thoughtfully. "I never touched the jewels until this evening when the butler handed them over to me. I honestly believed you had stolen them."

"I did not steal anything."

He made a disbelieving noise.

A twig snapped behind them, and she quickly spoke to distract him from the sound. "Why did you do it?"

He said meditatively, "Father insulted me often, hated me and always preferred Ian. But it wasn't hatred for my father that pushed me to do this. It was love. Love for the poor helpless animals in the world."

She nodded frantically encouraging him to go on.

ANYA WYLDE

He continued, "So many animals in this world need shelter, Miss Trotter. Surely you understand that. I have to feed them and give them all that they require. I want to travel and find the most beautiful creatures in the world and bring them home to live with me. And I couldn't do any of it unless this mansion was sold. And Father would not agree. He refused to sell it. I had to kill him," he finished passionately.

"I understand," she lied.

His grasp on her waist gentled. "I would have helped you run away, Miss Trotter, if only you had confided in me. It wouldn't have come to this. You could have set sail for France and had a fortune to spend. I could have sold this house, and everyone would have believed you had murdered my father. It would have been ideal."

"Please," she whispered, "you can still let me go. I will go to France. Run away from here. You don't have to kill me."

"I know you don't blame me. My pets . . . they know a good soul," he said softly. "I will miss you, Miss Trotter. But since you know the truth, I cannot risk letting you live." He sighed unhappily, "I will have to sacrifice you for the larger good. I know you understand . . . only you can. Come along, my love, and we will write that note. It's getting late."

She squeezed her eyes closed. This was her chance, and she prayed that whoever was following behind them was not the blasted baboon but an intelligent human being.

ANYA WYLDE

She looked towards the three stars twinkling in the sky and wondered if a fourth would be forming in a moment from now.

Heart thundering, she ignored Peter's tug on her waist and opened her mouth and screamed like a crazed banshee, "Look, a BLOOMING FLYING ELEPHANT!"

Peter looked.

Instantly her fingers flew to his nostril and rammed themselves in. Her elbow moved at the same time and slammed against his stomach.

"Oof," he exclaimed, and his hold on her slackened.

She ducked and twirled out of his grip in time to spot Lord Adair come flying towards Peter's wrist.

He grabbed Peter's hand and twisted it until his fingers spread in pain and the pistol fell out.

In a blink of an eye, Lord Adair held the pistol to Peter's defeated temple.

It all happened so fast that her head was left reeling. She dazedly watched Lord Adair tighten his hold on Peter's neck almost unable to believe that the real culprit had been nabbed and that she was free.

Lord Adair grinned and cocked an eyebrow at her. "Blooming elephant?"

"Flying elephant," Peter corrected in disgust.

"It worked, didn't it?" she asked, her knees sagging in relief.

"If only you hadn't said elephant," Peter growled, "I wouldn't have looked."

ANYA WYLDE

"I considered shouting yellow buffalo," she informed him.

"Blast it," Peter muttered and allowed Lord Adair to lead him away.

Chapter 35

It is incredible how the world view shifts along with the circumstances.

Yesterday Lucy was dreaming of catching pigeons and cooking them over flames in a dark part of a forest to survive, and today she was eyeing those very birds with a sort of motherly affection. She couldn't dream of dining on them. In fact, she found them positively endearing, fussing about on a branch with wings and things.

She strolled over to her favourite bench and perched her happy bottom on the sun-warmed wood. So much had changed in one day.

Life was funny like that.

You were rich one minute and poor the next or poor one moment and rich the next. It could go either way. And she was glad that this time life had changed directions in her favour.

She pulled out a cigar that she had pinched from the library and lit it. She didn't want to smoke it precisely but hold it in her hand, wave it about and look important. It felt like the right thing to do on such a joyous occasion.

She stared at the animal house through the haze of dancing cigar smoke. Last evening she had been ready to flee the manor with a single shawl and two pillows stuffed up her dress.

Last evening her skin had been chilled, her heart frightened and her nose so cold that she was surprised it hadn't fallen off at some point.

She sighed. Last evening had been eventful. After her own nightly adventure, Lord Adair had flowed onto the scene like a magician, woken the entire household and left every yawning head spellbound as he had explained Peter's deadly hand in the whole matter.

For once Lady Sedley had swooned convincingly. Elizabeth had paled and dug her nails into the sofa, leaving a momentous claw mark in the pink leather.

And as for Ian . . . Ian had heard the news, walked about, digested the fact that his brother was the culprit, and when the truth of it all finally penetrated his thick skull, he had started to sway, and he had continued to sway on his astonished legs until his eyes had begun to blur.

It was a long time before a sound passed his lips.

He had squeaked and snorted a few times before anyone realised he was trying to whistle.

And when he had finally managed to whistle, it had begun as a sweet little wobbly tune which soon turned into a full-fledged song of joy, love and ale.

ANYA WYLDE

He had leapt into the air, bounced a few times on chairs and tables and raced about the house like a five-year-old presented with a basket brimming full of sweets.

He had hugged and kissed every single person in the house and glowed like a dewy sunflower, and all because he had realised that he now owned not only the jewels but also the whole blasted manor.

Lucy had not waited around to hear the rest of it . . . That is, she had wanted to but was ordered to retire to her room by Elizabeth.

And tragically she hadn't been allowed to eavesdrop either.

She had lain awake for hours, mulling over the horrifying discovery that a baboon had killed poor old Lord Sedley.

And Lord Adair, she smiled, had stood by the truth even though the culprit had turned out to be an aristocrat.

She flicked the ash from the cigar just as she had seen Lord Adair do and took a thoughtful puff.

And if last night had been eventful, then this morning had been no less exciting.

She had walked into the kitchen to find hot sweet tea and warm breakfast waiting for her on the table. The servants had watched her consume one egg and part of sausage before erupting into a babble of apologies.

The cook had sobbed into her handkerchief and handed Lucy two cakes, a fresh loaf of bread and a pot of jam.

Lucy had hugged the cook in delight, who had enthusiastically squeezed her back until Lucy had almost choked to death.

The butler informed her that he and the scullery maid were getting married. She had been cordially invited to the wedding. He was planning to retire and open an inn with the money Lord Sedley had left him.

In turn, the scullery maid had blushed a whole lot, and between fits of giggles, enthusiastically pumped Lucy's hand, and given her an excellent recipe for Brunswick Black and blessed her with ever shining rust-free grates.

Rose had shuffled up to her next. Dear feisty Rose, with her adorable garbled accent of part French, part Russian and a smattering of Irish. She had sternly apologised for her bad behaviour and demanded forgiveness. Her voice dipped a touch and trembled when she mentioned the delicate matter where she had threatened to bite off Lucy's sweet little nose.

Tears had sprung up in Lucy's eyes at the confession, and she had warmly embraced the robust woman.

Rose, in turn, had stood like a lump, gritted her teeth and allowed this display of physical affection for a change.

Then it had been time for goodbyes.

At this point, everyone had burst into noisy tears, including the butler. Hiccups, sobs and the sound of servants blowing their noses had resounded in the kitchen.

Lucy had been touched, and she cried like she had never cried before. She had howled and howled and howled, prompting a wolf in the animal house to respond.

But it was the cook who outshone them all. She displayed grief like a tragic soul, an artist on stage or a frequent visitor of funerals. If Lucy's tears could have filled a large kettle, then the cook's tears caused the kitchen to flood. Soon every boot in the room had been soaked by the cook's salty tears . . .

"Questions skipping about in your head?"

She looked up to find Lord Adair standing in front of her. The sun seemed to form a halo around his head.

"Will you answer them?" she asked.

"Gladly," he replied. "Shall we stroll while we palaver?"

"Jabber," she said, standing up, "not palaver."

He pressed his lips together.

"Now, my lord," she asked, "when did you know that the baboon did it?"

"Do you recall that day when you had disguised yourself as a bush and were tailing Lady Sedley? You had come close to discovering the truth. A few feet away from where you stood eavesdropping on Lady Sedley and Peter's conversation, concealed inside the old stables, was the dummy wearing Lord Sedley's old clothes."

"I was disguised as a tree, not a bush," she corrected him. "Why didn't you unmask the plot that very day, my lord?"

"If I had told the family that a baboon killed Lord Sedley and the only clue I had was a giant doll, would anyone have believed me?"

"Sounds loony," she conceded.

They circled around a large puddle of muddy water whose surface was shimmering with the colours of the rainbow.

"What will Elizabeth do now?" Lucy asked.

"She has decided to go to London. An old aunt of hers lives there and owns a modest house. Elizabeth will take care of her aunt while planning a season in London."

"Ian and Lady Sedley will be going to Bath?" she prompted.

"Yes," he replied quietly. "And I will return to Lockwood."

"Yes, well . . . ." She trailed off.

"I should return indoors. I have some small matters to see to before departing."

"Wait, one last question."

He hesitated.

"Please," she coaxed.

He smiled and gestured for her to continue.

"What happened to the valet?"

"He escaped last night."

"And the jewels . . . Who had placed them in my room?"

"You already asked your last question."

"I promise no more after this one. Tell me who placed the jewels in my room."

The smile widened. "Why, I did, Miss Trotter. I put the box of jewels on your bed."

Her mouth dropped open. She asked slowly, "You stole the jewels from Elizabeth's room and placed them in mine?"

He bowed in response.

She stamped a small foot. "Why the devil would you do such a thing?"

"Calm the anger spinning atop your nose, Miss Trotter. I wanted everyone to be certain that the crimes had been committed by you."

"Why you—"

"I wanted to lull Peter into a false sense of security, and once he relaxed, he made the mistake I was waiting for."

"You used me," she fumed.

"I did what I could to save you." He shrugged and tipped his hat at her. "Goodbye, Miss Trotter."

"I won the bet," she said to his departing back.

He froze.

She lifted her skirts and hurried after him. "I caught the murderer before you did. Or rather, he caught me, but catching has been done, and I was involved first, so I win."

She impatiently brushed aside a branch and leapt over a large rock. "Did you hear what I said, my lord? Stop walking so fast. Wait a moment, Lord Adair. You and I have unfinished business. Stop, I say, you blasted man!"

ANYA WYLDE

Chapter 36

Lucy sourly watched the bags being carried into the waiting carriage.

The gold Lockwood family crest of an eagle and Pegasus soaring over a friendly-looking lion glinted in the sun every time the door was opened and closed by Lord Adair's valet.

She heaved her own small bag up on the step and sat down to wait.

"He will have to take me with him," she told the kittens in the basket.

They mewed sceptically.

A soft sob to her right made her turn her head.

She could see no one, and yet the pathetic crying continued. "Who is it?"

"It is I," Aunt Sedley howled.

Lucy squinted harder and finally saw a brief outline of a translucent ghost. "Aunt Sedley?"

"I am not your aunt," Aunt Sedley wept.

"I am sorry, I had gotten used to thinking . . . Oh, you are so sweet."

"Eh?"

"You are crying because I am leaving. You are going to miss me," Lucy said, touched.

"No, you daft fool. The wedding," Aunt Sedley yowled, "is off."

"Why the devil?"

"Mr Brown had a Mrs Brown hidden away. The spirits in charge of the wedding found out all about it." The ghost sobbed and blew her nose. "Mr Brown thought that after death, all familial ties were over, but the spirits in charge said no such luck. He continues to be married to Mrs Brown, whether he likes it or not, for the next seven generations."

"Who are the spirits in charge?"

"Who the bloody hell cares," Aunt Sedley bewailed. "I am not getting married, that is the point. I no longer want to live anywhere near Blackwell village. I never want to haunt the streets that I haunted with him. I want to go far, far away."

"You can leave the mansion?"

"Don't ask foolish questions," Aunt Sedley hiccuped.

"What are you going to do?"

"Wibble wibble gibbble."

"What?"

"Wiggle riggble akh."

"Please stop blubbering for a moment," Lucy begged. "I cannot understand a word."

"Will you," Aunt Sedley sniffed, "take me with you?"

"I don't know where I am going."

"I thought you were going with Lord Adair."

"I have to convince him yet."

"But he is leaving any moment now," the spirit exclaimed.

"I know. I am going to try one last time, and if not, then I will have to go to an inn, take a room for a few days and hunt around for employment."

Aunt Sedley stopped crying. "You don't have references."

"No, and if I tell them who my previous employers were, they will hear of the murder and theft—"

"And assume you had a hand in it," Aunt Sedley finished.

"Besides, Lord Adair knows everyone in England. No one will question him if he decides to employ me or asks someone else to give me work."

"He has to take you along."

"I hope he does," Lucy sighed.

"You know," Aunt Sedley said thoughtfully, "he will always be the hero."

"And I the heroine," she replied dreamily.

"You, my dear, are a side character."

"Hmmph."

"I have always wanted to see Lockwood," Aunt Sedley said, perking up after a moment. "Lord Adair had several handsome and powerful ancestors. Some may still be floating around in the halls."

"I don't doubt it."

"I may meet someone new," Aunt Sedley said hopefully. "I will—"

The door opened, cutting Aunt Sedley short, and with a gust of wind, Lord Adair strode out. His long black travelling cloak swirled around him, and his shiny boots silently descended the steps.

"My lord," Lucy said, coming to stand before him. "It is time to honour our wager. You promised to give me some sort of employment if I won. "

"I had solved the crime before you even began to make sense of it," he replied dismissively. He searched the clear blue sky and turned to the valet. "It is a good day for travelling. Don't forget the balloon—"

"You managed to catch Peter," she cut in, "but you had to use me to get to him. You might need me again."

"I doubt it."

"I am willing to learn."

"I have nothing to teach."

"You cannot abandon me, I have nowhere to go."

"You can return to the orphanage."

"They won't have me."

"I can offer you coins to survive until you find yourself some suitable employment."

"I am no beggar."

He shrugged and gracefully entered the carriage.

She caught hold of the door. "You found a home for Palmer, the chickens, the frogs, the rats and even that horrid evil Egyptian bird. Surely you can find something for me."

"You are not a helpless little pug, Miss Trotter, that I can hand over to a bunch of greedy children," he said and rapped the carriage walls, "or a remarkable specimen for some old medical professor to mull over."

"But I am a girl of gentle disposition. I am educated. I can play the piano, the harpsichord, the flute. I can write exquisite letters, speak French and argue like a Greek philosopher. I can knit, sew, paint and dance. I can bake divine little cakes light as air, my loaves of bread can satisfy even the king. I can mop, dust and frighten away wrinkles," she cried as the carriage started to roll away.

"I know how to prise a bullet out of a man and make a salve for a nasty cut," she continued, running alongside the moving carriage. "I know how to use the Hunga Munga, the lethal African fighting tool. I can brawl like an experienced street urchin and keep the fawning women away from you, Lord Adair."

The carriage quickened its pace, and she could no longer keep up.

"I am immune to your charms, my lord," she screamed in one last desperate attempt.

The carriage jerked to a reluctant halt, and Lord Adair's head poked out. He said resignedly, "Come along then, Miss Trotter."

Lucy grinned in triumph. She threw the small cloth bag over her shoulder, grasped the basket of mewing kittens and with Spinoza the raven securely perched upon her bonnet hurtled towards the carriage.

The ghost of Aunt Sedley whooped in delight and whizzed after her.

They both leapt in, ghost and human, and settled opposite the handsomest man on earth, Lord William Ellsworth Hartell Adair, the Marquis of Lockwood.

Aunt Sedley produced a glass of champagne and sipped the ghostly bubbles. "To a new beginning and yet another spirited adventure," she toasted.

"Amen to that," Lucy sighed happily and settled down for the long ride ahead.

The End

If you enjoyed this book, then please check out Anya Wylde's other releases on Amazon.

About the Author

Anya Wylde lives in Ireland along with her husband and a fat French poodle (now on a diet). She can cook a mean curry, and her idea of exercise is occasionally stretching her toes. She holds a degree in English literature and adores reading and writing.

To be the first to hear of any new releases by Anya Wylde email her at anyawylde@gmail.com

Copyright:
This work is copyright. Apart from any use as permitted under the Copyright Act 1968, no part maybe reproduced, copied, scanned, stored in a retrieval system, recorded or transmitted, in any form or by any means, without the prior written permission of the publisher.
This book is a work of fiction. Names, characters, places and incidents are either a product of the author's imagination or are used fictitiously. Any resemblance to actual people living or dead, events or locales is entirely coincidental.